LUST JIHAD

Priya A Gaikwad

Leadstart
INKSTATE

ISBN
Copyright © Priya Gaikwad, 2020

First published in India 2021 by Leadstart Inkstate
A Division of One Point Six Technologies Pvt Ltd

Sales Office:
Unit No.25/26, Building No.A/1,
Near Wadala RTO,
Wadala (East), Mumbai – 400037 India
Phone: +91 969933000
Email: info@leadstartcorp.com
www.leadstartcorp.com

Disclaimer: The views expressed in this book are those of the Author and do not pertain to be held by the Publisher.

Editor: Kavya Shree
Cover: Sushant Bhosle
Layouts: Kshitij Dhawale

About the Author

Priya Gaikwad is a professor teaching Mass Media for the last four years. Her creators believe that she lives inside Netflix, Hotstar and Amazon Prime oblivious to the world around her (which is true).

Her nephew, niece, family and students are her world. When not reading, writing or binge-watching shows, you'll find her sleeping, forming a new story in her head.

Acknowledgements

I am forever grateful to the mistakes I've made in the past and the unknown force because of which this story was possible.

Contents

Part I

Chapter One

If you ask me to describe my feelings for him, I would like to quote this line I once read on the internet: *The way I feel for you, I could start fires with it.* Yes, that's how I feel for him; that's how I felt for him when I first saw him. I could not take my eyes off that gorgeous, smiling face. I knew I wanted him. I wanted him more than a dying man would want his life back. I told my gods: either you give me him or take my life.

What I got was way worse than I had imagined. I only saw the beautiful face and failed to realize what horror lay within him.

His name meant 'gift of god' and he indeed was a gift from god to me. I met him again, after one whole year at my cousin's wedding. Sahil, my cousin was getting married to his girlfriend, Meera, in three weeks. It was a grand wedding as Meera was an only child. My maternal uncle had booked two villas for all the ceremonies and we were to be present for each and every one of them.

"Hello," greeted Sahil as we entered the large villa after travelling for two hours from our house.

The villa had grown old and stood in the middle of nowhere like a grumpy old man. Few men were working to make it look like a beautiful bride. Hanging from the window, they decorated every corner with flowers and garlands.

"Congratulations," I chimed looking at my brother's handsome face which was glowing more than usual.

"Thank you," he smiled, hugging me. "I so need your support. You know I'm kind of…"

"Feeling scared?" I asked as many other people, known, unknown emerged from upstairs. "Cold feet?"

Noise, laughter, chatter filled the place as more people came down.

"Oh, shut up," he laughed nervously and I knew he was scared.

"I wish I could drink," he said as a group of aunties came downstairs adding to the decibel level.

"But you can't," I grinned, looking at my uncle who was busy introducing people to my parents.

"So when is Adi returning from Malaysia?" he asked diverting from the topic. Adi is my older brother, married and with a son.

"He will be there in two weeks," I informed as my eyes shifted to a group of people who looked unfamiliar and different.

"Oh, they are dad's friends from Kashmir." Sahil whispered close to my ears and I nodded.

And then *he* came down the stairs looking exactly like he used to. Thin, lanky, walking like a giraffe, dirty stubble, fair, babyish face, and haunting eyes.

"This is Ahyan," my uncle was telling my father while my mother got busy with aunties.

"What happened?" Sahil asked noticing my dazed face and open mouth. "You okay?"

"Hmm?" I asked distracted and openly staring at him. Ahyan noticed me too and looked shocked as well.

"Do you like him?" my brother teased and I felt his eyes on me.

"Yes," I whispered and moved my reluctant eyes to him. "Um, what? No. Who is he?"

"Ahyan," Sahil said just as his phone rang. "One of dad's friends' son. They are very close to each other." I nodded. "Oh shit, Meera is calling." He continued blabbering something while I gazed at Ahyan.

Finally, both my brother and Ahyan left. My mother had told me to find a room for myself and change my clothes.

Most of the rooms were already occupied and I finally found one at the end of the floor. As I was pushing my bag inside, I saw Ahyan going upstairs. Throwing the bag inside like it was a toy, I locked the door and ran after him. He entered a room on the 2nd floor and left the door slightly ajar. The windows were open and I could see him as he threw his phone on the bed and removed his white *kurta*.

Shamelessly, I pushed the door gently. He was already half naked and shocked to see me there.

"Ria?" he murmured and I felt the familiar joy in my stomach when I heard my name from his lips.

"What are you doing here?" he asked nervously. "Someone might catch us."

"Oh, yes," I nodded and closed the door, locking it. "Fine?"

"Ria," he again murmured my name putting the *kurta* back on. "I don't think you should be here."

"Then where should I be?" I asked still standing by the door and gazing at him, drinking him through my eyes.

"It's been a year," he gasped sitting on the bed. "I had forgotten everything…"

"I haven't," I blurted, my eyes wet, hands shaking. I couldn't believe he could utter those words out of his beautiful mouth. Had he forgotten everything? Had he forgotten me? How?

"Come here," he called me in that husky voice which had me melted back in college.

I sat beside him on the bed and we decided to let the silence do the talking.

"So, how are you?" he finally asked and I smiled sadly, now crying with tears streaming down my face.

"Fine," I nodded wiping the tears. "It took time to pick up the pieces but… I did fine."

"I'm sorry," he replied, hurt visible in his tone. "I don't know what to say…"

"Don't say anything," I muttered, eyes still wet. "Your words won't bring back anything and neither will it erase my pain."

"Aww! I'm so sorry, Ria." He leaned forward for his classic move—put his hands around my shoulder and arrest me from everywhere.

"Don't!" I yelled yanking his hand away. "You don't get to touch me, Ahyan. You lost every right to touch me when you left."

"But Ria… Please try and understand…" before he could start the whole saga someone knocked on the door.

I had to hide in the washroom, where his underwear was hanging, till his father left the room.

While in the washroom, my pocket started vibrating, indicating torture—my mother was calling.

"Gotta go." I burst out of the washroom, ignoring his pleas for me to stay.

All ten families were staying in the two villas, including Meera's. Ahyan had to share his room with his father; his mother was in Kashmir because Ahyan's *naani* was ill, and few uncles who were my uncle's friends. As for me, I was sharing my room with two of Meera's friends and my cousin Veera, whom I despised. Veera was three years older and was always a bitch to everyone since childhood. Unlike others, I wore my hatred on my face. She had been married for a year and her husband was to join the wedding party in a few days.

"So, Ria…?" she said while unpacking her stuff at night. Sonam and Anushka, Meera's friends, were busy on their phones. "Sahil is same age as you, right?" I looked at her with disinterest and decided not to answer the bitch.

"He is getting married," she continued as I focused on my book. "What's going on with you? Any guy in your life?"

"None of your business," I muttered still reading the book.

"But people will question you." She plopped herself next to me. "Sahil being a guy is getting married at 26, then why not you Ria?" Batting her eyelashes she waited for an answer.

"Once my boyfriend gets out of jail, we will marry," I replied with a smug smile as Sonam and Anushka laughed at my joke.

Veera did not take it well and left the room fuming.

The next day by the time I arrived at the dining room, most people had already eaten. I found Sonam staring at her food intently like it was a math problem.

"What happened?" I asked, dropping a *naan* in my plate.

"Too much oil *yaar!*" she said with a sad face and moved towards salad.

I laughed and leaned forward to get a pickle when I felt someone's hand on my ass. Instantly, I turned around and found the *lamppost* behind me.

"Ahyan…" I merely whispered as many of my aunts were sitting on a couch near the dining table.

He didn't say anything and collected his plate smiling.

"Uh, hmm," rang a familiar voice in my ears which belonged to my brother. "Dear sister, can I talk to you?"

"What?" I asked. Sahil took me outside, near the balcony from where we could see aunties hanging clothes on the terrace.

"What was going on there?" he asked casually and I shrugged. "Do you know Ahyan?"

"Um, what? No." I looked down immediately because Sahil was one of the people I could never lie to easily.

"You know him," he said loudly as a few aunties dining inside frowned at us. "You know him?" he whispered this time as I folded my hands in front of him, begging him to keep it down.

"Oh my god," he muttered looking down and then at me with horror dancing in his eyes. "He is that guy! He is the same Muslim guy you were crazy for a few months back?"

I didn't say anything and stared at his face, nodding once.

"Ria," he spoke in his brotherly tone, "You do remember what you went through then? I remember how much you suffered and were humiliated. And I'm pretty sure you do too."

"Yes," I whispered still feeling the humiliation Adi had caused me.

"Then why to go forward with it again?" he touched my arm. "You are a very sensible girl. Why would you bring this suffering upon yourself?"

"Sahil…" I found it difficult to put my thoughts into words, gasping, I controlled my tears. "I want to suffer. I cannot lose him this time."

Sahil stared at me for a few minutes and then nodded. "Okay. But whatever you do…just be careful and do not get caught this time."

"I won't," I assured him as he flashed me a smile. Next second his phone started ringing and he had to run to his bridezilla.

I didn't go back to my food but stood there watching children play on the terrace. Instantly, I was sucked back into the past and remembered everything like it had happened yesterday.

I met Ahyan in college. He was my senior and I was a clueless 18-year-old. The first time I saw him I got a funny feeling all through my body. A feeling you get when you see lust walking towards you. Unable to understand what it was, I shunned him and my feelings away. I never spoke to him, avoided him and was almost invisible when he was near me.

But we met again 6 years later. I had started working as an academic counsellor and he was working as an event manager. We happened to meet at a party and by then I was aware of what I felt for him. I didn't waste any time in letting him know about my fantasies and my desires. He smiled at first when I told him everything like I was narrating a story.

Since we used to be pretty busy, we spoke mostly on calls. My hormones could not understand certain things and I was losing my mind. I could not work properly, hardly slept at home, stopped eating and usually spent my time daydreaming. My body would not listen to me.

We met three times, out of which only once we could touch each other. Even though he was rough, I wanted more. That's when we decided to arrange for a place. My brother Aditya got hold of my messages and read everything. It wasn't enough that I was planning to sleep with a guy out of wedlock, but that guy also happened to be a Muslim.

My mother tortured me for days and kept taunting me that I had tainted the family name by talking to a Muslim guy. Thankfully, my father was out of town so he had no idea what his dear daughter had done. Frankly, I had not done anything; I had only kissed him and let him touch me. We had not crossed any line; we were adults and knew what we were doing.

To make things worse, my brother called Ahyan and threatened him to stay away from me. Fortunately, no one knew what he looked like. Ahyan too advised me that we should listen to my family. I got mad, madder at Ahyan than my family. I begged him not to leave me like this, but he had made up his mind.

I abused him, called him names and told him to never show his face again. My words, to be precise, were, "Fuck off, Ahyan. I never dreamt that you would chicken out like this. You are a fucking pussy."

I never heard from him again.

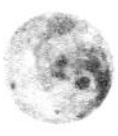

I did not go back to the dining room for lunch. I ran to my room, locked myself up and cried. When I came out it was already dinner time and my mother was yelling at me to come out.

The dining room was full of people. Some were seated while others, like my father, were standing by the window and eating. My phone vibrated signalling a text.

I had 40 messages from Ahyan. Before I could reply I saw him entering the room. All of us sat laughing, smiling and talking as servants served us food. Ahyan was sitting opposite to me and my mother was talking to my aunts.

All of a sudden she started talking to Ahyan's dad and our eyeballs popped out.

"Yes *bhaisaab*," she said flashing an innocent smile, "we want to visit Kashmir once. When do you think will be an ideal time?"

His dad started blabbering something while I tried my hardest not to look at him directly. An aunty sitting beside me got a call and disappeared towards the balcony. Hearing that my mother was making plans my dad took the vacated seat.

"*Toh aap pehle* Kashmir *main rehte the?*" asked my dad as he took a spoonful of his dessert.

His father smiled and nodded. Ahyan's family lived in Kashmir till he was 10 and that's when my uncle, who used to often visit Kashmir, met his father. They moved here later, to the city of dreams, where Ahyan pursued his education.

"Ahyan was not ready to come to the wedding. In fact, he told me he is leaving after tomorrow's ceremony." I purposely dropped the fork which fell with a loud clatter.

My dad picked it up for me while I stared at my plate.

"Um, no *Abu*," Ahyan muttered, "I'm going to stay. I spoke to my boss and he said I can join after three weeks."

"But you said you wanted to go and see your *naani* too," added his dad. My uncle, meanwhile, filled my mother in about his *naani*'s health.

"I will definitely go and meet her later," he promised, flashing his boyish smile.

My father started inquiring about life in Kashmir and my mother asked how Ahyan's *naani* was. It was funny how someone who could not tolerate the fact that I met a Muslim guy was taking interest in his family. Talk about hypocrisy.

Having finished my dinner, I went to wash my hands. Apart from a few children, there was no one on the ground floor. Ahyan grabbed my hand and forced me inside a bathroom.

"What you doing?" I asked as his hands groped me everywhere. His stubble was poking me once again. He had already unzipped my *kurta* from behind as I was struggling to stop his large hands from sneaking inside my dress.

"Ahyan, *stop!*" I screamed but he covered my mouth with his hand.

"Don't scream," he whispered in my ears, nuzzling my cheek.

I removed his hand from my mouth and let out a sigh. "What the fuck are you doing?" I asked angrily as he struggled to unhook my bra.

"Fucking you," he replied coolly as I yanked his hand away from my dress.

"No, you are not," I replied pushing him back. "Not here, Ahyan!"

"What, why?" He sounded mad and shocked.

I adjusted my dress and glared at him. "I have waited a long time for this and I'm not doing it in this stupid, stinking bathroom."

"Okay," he nodded looking at the shabby place. "I'll clean it if you want?"

"No way," I yelled again trying to zip up my *kurta* but could not reach the zipper.

"*Oh come on*, Ria," he said again coming closer to me but I warned him not to touch me.

"No means no, Ahyan," I fumed as he bottled up his anger.

"Fine then," he gritted his teeth and shot a dangerous look at me.

"At least help me zip up the dress," I said but he was already gone.

I rolled my eyes and laughed thinking how certain things never change.

Next day, during the engagement ceremony, I was dressed in a pink *ghagra* which was too loose for my thin body. I looked like a hanger and decided to hide this flaw by wearing too many accessories.

My brother looked handsome, dressed in a maroon *sherwani*, whereas Meera was dressed in an onion coloured *saree*. They both looked happy and real.

I could not take my eyes off another thin body dressed in a white *kurta* and black jacket. I kept smiling at everyone so that whenever my eyes fell on him I would smile at him too. But he stared mildly at me.

Finally, when the lovebirds exchanged rings, my mother ordered me to distribute sweets to everyone. I took Sonam with me even though Veera wanted to help. I offered Ahyan's dad some, which he took joyfully. When I offered the box to Ahyan, he gave me an *are-you-fucking-me* look.

"*Le lo*, Ahyan," ordered his dad and went back to talking to someone.

"*Nahi chahiye*," he stated dryly, removing his phone from his pocket.

I slapped his hand hard which made him drop his phone. He looked like he would eat me and spit me out.

"I'm so sorry," I apologized and handed him the box. "I will get your phone..." I smiled at some aunties who caught our attention but then went back to talking about their *sarees*.

I purposely readjusted the *dupatta* so my breasts would be on display for him. Since the dress was loose, he couldn't see anything till I leaned towards him.

"Hmm, your phone," I said while his eyes looked back at me in shock. "Want some sweets?" I asked innocently.

"No," he replied, handing me the box and going red.

"Okay," I nodded and pulled my *dupatta* down again.

I wanna meet you.
I wanna do you. Now.

My phone was flooded with similar messages after the *dupatta* dropping scene. I wanted to laugh out loud but could not in front of my mother. One of my youngest cousins did ask me why I was giggling so much.

Ahyan's face was filled with so many emotions. At one point, I could not understand if he was angry or just horny. At night we—Sonam, Anushka, and even Veera—were busy texting our respective men.

I wanna do it, said Ahyan's message again and I checked the time. 12:30am.

But place?

You just come down. I will find us someplace.

No. Are you mad? What if someone catches us?

I rolled my eyes as I hit send.

No one will na baby. Plz.

Be practical, Ahyan.

Arey, I'm being practical. No one will catch us.

You are being stupid.

I just wanna fuck you. Please come to me.

And what will happen if anyone catches us in the act?

Oh, let them.

Wow! Look at you. Suddenly no fear of family.

What does that mean?

You very well know what it means.

You are taunting me?

Of course, since you always keep thinking about family. What happened now? Dick overpowering brain?

Needless to say, I was a little annoyed.

Huh. Maybe.

Well, you kept me hanging; maybe this is how god is punishing you now.

What?

You know what.

Huh.

Classic Ahyan. Like I didn't know his secret codes. He would send me a 'Huh' when he was furiously mad at me.

He didn't reply and I too decided to stop torturing myself and slept.

Next day, I didn't get any messages either. I looked for him but he was nowhere to be seen. My aunt asked me to get some old curtains from the storage room. It took me ages to locate the room which was in the backyard of the villa. I was busy looking for the curtains when I heard someone open the door. Ahyan was already locking it shut behind shut before I could open my mouth.

"What was that last night, huh?" he said angrily, his eyes flaming fire.

"Um, what?" I stammered realizing I was still scared of his temper.

"That I left you and stuff," he muttered as I finally saw some curtains placed on an old stool near a window.

"It's true, isn't it?" I asked moving towards the stool but he blocked me.

"There was a reason why I did what I did," he replied glaring at me.

"Whatever," I shrugged casually. "You left me."

"You will always be a kid, Ria," he shook his head and moved closer. "Everything is not an adventure. You cannot be a rebel all the time."

"I was not asking you to start a revolution," I screamed, annoyed now. "I was just asking you to fuck me like you were asking me last night."

"And what? Get caught?" he asked crossing his hands against his chest.

"How the fuck were you going to get caught?" I retorted crossly. "I was the one who put everything at stake. My family knew everything about us and yet I wanted to give us a chance. Your family had no idea what had happened and yet you chickened out. You behaved like a fucking pussy."

His face turned even more dangerous than I had ever seen. I knew the word would affect him and I purposely used it again.

"Don't call me that again," he murmured, warning me under his breath looking down at me.

"Why?" I laughed. "Stings? Is that why you never replied to me? Because I hurt your ego?"

"Enough," he looked up and his eyes told me to stop it right there. Like I was going to.

"You were a pussy, Ahyan," I repeated the words with tears in my eyes and moved towards the stool.

He caught hold of my hand and slammed me against the wall. Even though he was thinner than me, he was strong.

We stared at each other as I struggled to get out of his clutch.

"What the fuck, Ahyan!?" I cried out but he didn't budge. "What are you doing?"

"This," he said and kissed me.

Memories from our first kiss came back. How much I hated it. How uncoordinated it was.

Finally, I pushed him back. "Ughh! Ahyan!" I wiped my chin with the back of my sleeve. "Again the same old thing!" I whined as he looked at me in confusion. "Why the fuck can't you use your lips? Why do you have to exploit my mouth with your stupid tongue?"

"What?" he was shocked as he wiped his own mouth.

"Use your lips," I repeated and picked up the curtains. "I hate it when you just stick your tongue down my throat."

"But you never told me back then…"

"I'm telling you now," I replied.

Someone knocked on the door and we both froze.

"Ssshh!" he put his finger on his lips and pressed his ear against the door.

"It's Akram *chacha*," he whispered to me as I started looking for a place to hide.

"Ahyan, *darwaza kholo*," his uncle yelled. "*Jaldi…*"

"Um, *haan*," he replied as I opened the window and decided to take a jump.

"*Ek* minute *haan*," said Ahyan and helped me out the window.

"Sorry," he muttered and slammed the window shut in my face.

I stood there holding the curtains and looking around at the cows and the well.

When I turned around, I spotted Anushka and Sonam waving at me. They were hiding behind a tree smoking. I waved back and joined them.

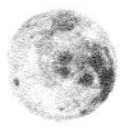

At night, everyone was gathered downstairs checking out the pictures from the ceremonies. Ahyan kept calling me on my phone so I decided to take escort in my room and talk to him privately.

When I reached my room, he disconnected the phone abruptly.

"Hey, check out the pictures," I heard a voice from Veera's bed where she was sitting with few of my other cousins. "They are so beautiful."

"Um, weren't you people checking out pictures downstairs?" I asked sitting on my bed.

"No," said Sita, my youngest cousin who was Veera's *chamchi*. "We clicked so many pics on Veera di's phone. They look much better. See, we got yours too."

"Oh yeah," Veera looked at me with her snake eyes painted with *kajal*. "Check this out," handing me the phone she sneered, "Beautiful, no? But where is your attention? Where exactly are you looking?"

I scanned the picture carefully and realized that I was looking towards my left where Ahyan was sitting. Thankfully, he was not caught in the frame, but Veera certainly noticed something strange.

"I was looking at the ceremony," I replied with a smug smile.

"Oh yes, the ceremony." She added with a smile, "The ceremony was quite interesting."

Before I could answer my phone began ringing. I picked it up and marched out of the room.

I heard her laughing behind me. "Ceremony calling."

"What?" I whispered standing in the corridor. "Hello?"

"Come to the terrace. Now," he murmured from the other end. I wanted to yell my lungs out that how the fuck could he call me at the terrace now?

"But?" was all I managed to mutter.

"Come. Quick," he pleaded. "We got no time. Move your fucking ass *now*."

With that, he disconnected. I looked everywhere twice and ran upstairs.

I found few of my cousins and relatives as well as Meera's playing cricket. Ahyan was standing near the entrance and pretended I was invisible. Finally, after a minute or two he disappeared behind a huge water tank.

After my cousin Amit got out, everyone started booing him. I followed Ahyan as no one was paying heed to us.

"Why did you call me here?" I whispered, stressed. "What if somebody—"

"Shh!!" he placed his long finger on my lips. "Don't talk."

"Then?" I whispered from behind his fingers.

"I'm sorry for whatever happened down there." I smiled as he continued, "And I wanted to give you something." Finally, he removed his finger from my lips.

"What?" I asked again and he kissed my lips gently.

"This is what you wanted, right?" he asked cheekily and I blushed, nodding my head slowly.

"It's good, isn't it?" I asked and kissed his lips again.

"Uh…" he shrugged as if bored. I pushed him away, laughing.

"Out!" We heard someone yell and I asked Ahyan to join them. He was reluctant at first but then he saw my father bowling and agreed.

I stood behind the tank and watched him play with my father happily. Rings of smoke emerging from behind the other tank caught my interest as I sneaked there and found my brother smoking.

"What's up?" I asked and he jumped, almost throwing the cigarette down.

"You scared me!" he said his eyes going twice their usual size. "So, where's your lover boy?"

"He is out there, playing cricket with my father." I asked him for a cigarette.

"You guys are going really strong, huh?" he asked as I lit my cigarette poorly.

He pulled it from my mouth and lit the monster properly before passing it to me. "Strong is a strong word. We are just exploring things, no pressure on each other."

"That's cool too," he smiled. "Take your own time and enjoy."

"How are things with you?" I asked and his face had many emotions which I found difficult to register.

"Little scary," he admitted openly like always. "But then…I imagine our lives together, the joy on her face, her gorgeous face," he smiled sweetly, unlike many guys, "and things cool down."

"You are lucky," I replied taking a puff and he agreed.

"You too seem happy with Ahyan," he pointed out and I agreed. "I can see the happiness on your face. The way you glow when he is around. I hope it stays that way forever."

I laughed and rolled my eyes, "Thanks, bro."

"I don't think he is out," I heard my dad screaming. Both Sahil and I popped our heads out and found my father defending Ahyan as he asked my dad to bat.

Chapter Two

It was the *Mehndi* ceremony and the ladies were busting their asses to get the work done so they could decorate their hands.

In the morning, during breakfast, Ahyan passed me a plate. Even though our parents were seated near us, we stayed close to each other. I took the plate and found that on the tissue he had written something.

I looked closely and it read: 'I wanna do it.'

I rolled my eyes and stuffed the tissue in my *kurta's* pocket. Throughout breakfast he kept mouthing at me *I wanna do it*. I was terrified someone would catch us but no one noticed except Veera.

Finally, in the afternoon when the ceremony began, I excused myself and lied to my mother that I needed to take a bath as I was feeling very hot. Running to his room, I texted him that I was coming. He was already alone. His uncles and father had gone for a walk.

"I'm here," I panted closing the door after me. "I got only 20 minutes, babe. You think it's enough?"

"More than enough," he smiled pulling me close to him.

"Ahyan," I moaned as he undressed me, kissing my neck.

"Where is the condom?" I asked as he removed his shirt.

"Wait," he ordered and jumped from the bed to open the wardrobe.

"Be quick. I will get naked in the meanwhile." I said getting ready to remove my *kurta*.

"No. Wait!" he screamed, startling me as he laughed a little. "I mean, I will undress you."

"Hurry then. Get the fucking condom!" I yelled, checking the time as his head disappeared inside the wardrobe.

"What happened?" I asked after five minutes. He had finished checking the entire wardrobe.

"I don't remember where I kept it." Frustrated, he stood in front of me.

"Are you fucking with me?" I groaned. "Are you sure you had them?"

"Yes, I brought them the day I saw you," he answered in haste, not even noticing my reaction, "and I kept it somewhere here…but everyone is sharing these rooms and its causing confusion."

"Fuck that. What are we supposed to do now?" I bellowed at him right as my phone vibrated. "Wow," I checked the screen and danger was already calling.

"I gotta go, Ahyan," I got up, disappointed. "Mom's calling."

"Baby please," he begged pulling my hand towards him and kissing it.

"Sorry. No," I moaned. "We lost our chance. This always happens. I think something tells me we shouldn't be together."

"You remember when we were to meet for our first date, we faced so many problems and despite them, we met." I was already at the door. "Riaaa…"

"I'm going," I replied sadly and he looked at me as if someone had died. Or chewed on his dick.

"Hey," nudged Sonam as I was getting my *mehndi* done. "My boyfriend is going to come by with his old car. I asked him if he could lend it to us since we gotta pick things Meera ordered us to."

"Okay," I smiled and looked at the peacock that was being drawn on my hand. It looked more like a giant cock from where I saw. I shook my head and blinked several times.

"So, I and Anu are going to the market. You should join us too."

"I don't know…" I mused trying to find a comfortable position to straighten my back as I had been sitting without support for an hour.

"Well, you can drop us at the shop and then use the car." She then looked at me meaningfully and glanced where Ahyan was sitting with his father's friends and Sahil.

"What?" I shook my head, totally clueless.

"Come here," she ordered and I leaned forward. "I'm saying," she whispered, "you guys can do it in the car."

"What?" I almost yelled and caught my mother's attention. "Um, what?"

"Yeah," she winked. "Thank me later. Ranjit will be here in an hour. Be ready by then."

"How did you…?" I asked as my eyes wandered towards Ahyan who was watching me.

"Not important," she smiled. "Just be ready."

I laughed gazing at Ahyan. "We will be."

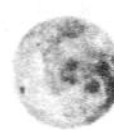

Finally at 5:00pm we were ready to visit the market to fetch Meera's blouse for the reception.

Sonam and Anushka were dropped near the auto stand and we took off in the old, yellow Santro towards a secluded area. It was mainly a jungle with strange birds singing.

The car stopped and my heart did too. I could not look at him even though I knew he was staring hungrily at me.

Putting his hand on my shoulders he pulled me closer. I could not breathe; it was so fucking stupid as I always wanted to be closer to him. But now, my insides were tickling with his touch.

"I think we should do it there," I said, eyeing the backseat.

"Why?" he whispered in my ears and kissed them, already in his sex trance.

Once Ahyan went in the sex trance it was difficult to shake him out and make him understand things. I held his jaw with my hand.

"Wait," I said and he looked disappointed and mad. "Let's go back there. It will be comfortable."

"Trust me, babe," he said sweetly, "we will be comfortable here too. Now, don't waste time. Come on."

"You are never going to listen to me, are you?" I muttered looking at my nails and he stormed out of the car.

Opening the rear door, he entered and waited for me. "Happy?"

I got out of the car, joining him. "Please don't be angry. I don't want you to be angry…"

"But I'm angry now," he retorted gritting his teeth and unzipping my t-shirt with one hand. "And I think you like me angry, huh?" He forced the shirt over my head and threw it at the steering wheel.

"Do you know how scared I get when you are angry, especially now, during sex?" I said almost trembling and he laughed.

"Sorry." He removed his shirt and threw it where it landed right on top of mine. "Let's do it, baby."

"Okay," I grinned but my phone started vibrating.

"Fuck! Don't tell me it's your mother," he exclaimed throwing his head back.

It was from my school. My head teacher was calling me.

"It's from school," I said unable to decide if I wanted to talk or not.

"Your students can wait," he unhooked the bra easily, putting it aside, "but I can't, baby."

I laughed and put the phone away as our pants came down.

"Please be gentle," I requested as he removed the condom which was mistakenly kept in his uncle's wardrobe. Thankfully, Ahyan found it before anyone else could.

"Yeah," he laughed sarcastically and kissed me, not with lips. My *mehndi* was completely ruined and for the first time ever I didn't care.

The wedding was in two days and all the ladies were busy with the *haldi* ceremony upstairs. We—Ahyan, Sonam, Anushka and I—sneaked out and decided to do our respective stuff. I and Ahyan were locked in the storage room, whereas Sonam and Anushka were busy smoking in the car.

The car had to be cleaned thoroughly before handing it to Sonam.

Of course, I did most of the cleaning while Ahyan kept grabbing for me.

"Ahyan," I said, trying to get his attention away from his phone.

"Hmm?" he murmured, rubbing his eyes.

"Will you teach me Urdu?" I asked dreamily and he stared at me.

"Why do you wanna learn Urdu?"

"I always wanted to." I pulled the phone from his hand. He was talking to a girl.

"Oh, who is this hot *chica*?" I asked and he snatched the phone from my hand.

"Co-worker."

"Hot," I said and asked him again. "Will you teach me Urdu?"

"Not if you keep pestering me," he answered with a smug.

"Fuck you then," I whispered and bit his stomach.

"Ouch!" He stared angrily at me. "That hurt…"

"So you do know what the word hurt means."

"What does that mean?" Angrily he put the phone down. "Huh?"

"I wanna learn Urdu," I repeated to change the topic as I did not want to fight. "I also wanna wear *burqa* once."

"You should," he pointed out sarcastically. "It will cover your nagging mouth. In fact, I think I saw one in my uncle's wardrobe that day. He must have brought my aunt's by mistake. Wanna wear it?"

"Really?" I got up from his lap triumphantly. "Of course! Bring it over, please."

He laughed then frowned. "I was kidding, Ria. But you really wanna wear it?"

"Yes," I smiled brightly. "You will be glad since it will cover my mouth and stuff…"

"Yeah." He got up, slapping his jeans to get the dirt off. "It's anyway useless…"

"Why?" I laughed. "Just because I won't blow you?"

"Yes," he replied and vanished to get the *burqa*.

Few minutes later, I finally saw myself in the *burqa*. Fragments of the broken mirror were lying in the storage room and I saw my unusual reflection in them. He was still on the phone while I could not take my eyes off of me.

"How do I look?" I asked and he finally kept the phone aside.

"Covered. Hidden. Smaller," he replied and disappointment filled inside me.

"You could have said something nice," I said angrily.

"Why?" he asked bossily. "Why should I lie? I tell the truth, always. I like you naked."

"Forget it," I shook my head. "Now come on, put you big hands to good use and click my pictures."

"What?" He sounded mad. It was difficult to understand why he was angry—because I ordered him to click my pictures or because of the hand comment.

"My phone's there," I pointed, "click few pictures of me." I stood in front of him smiling even though the heat was eating me up.

Ahyan wanted me to take off the *burqa* because he wanted to put it back in his uncle's wardrobe and he wanted to fuck in the storage room. I could not take it off. I felt like I was giving up a piece of my body. I don't know why I felt that way.

"Imagine if anyone catches us here?" I asked as we were lying naked on the dusty floor later.

"They will be shattered and scandalized," he laughed. "Give us crappy names. Term it as some kind of love jihad thing, specially your mother."

"What is Jihad, Ahyan?" I asked turning my face towards him.

"Well, Jihad is…not about killing innocents in the name of religion. The *holy war* has to first and foremost begin from within—against lies, corruption, temptation, the thought of oppressing the weak and also from turning away a blind eye when the weak and poor are being oppressed. Blowing your horn because you are brainwashed by some hate-monger doesn't earn you 72 virgins, instead, you bring disrepute, humiliation and extreme suffering to your own loved ones, the religion and the Beloved Prophet," he concluded as I stared at him in awe.

"Wow," I whispered, "I never knew you were this intelligent."

"*Achha*," he pulled me closer and bit my neck.

"If anyone ever catches us," I said hugging him, "I don't think they should term our relationship as Love Jihad as we don't love each other." We both bit our respective lips at that. "They should name it something fancier. Something like…Lust Jihad?"

Hearing that he burst out laughing, something he rarely did. "That is fascinating."

"Isn't it?" I asked blushing. "We have lusted after each other for years, so why not call us the Lust Jihadis."

"You know, the people who came up with the term Love Jihad would be ashamed that you came up with a cooler name," he said looking at me with a smile.

"Honey," I batted my eyelashes, "they will be so fucking traumatized that someone could come up with this term. And forget inventing the term, they would want to kill each other after they realize we are practicing what we preach."

"Oh yeah!" he laughed and nuzzled my nose. "Let's practice again."

"You need therapy," I said but he was already in the sex trance.

The next morning I was panicking as I had lost one of my 'family' earrings. It was given to me by my brother during his wedding. I had a bad feeling that it was either lost in the storage room or was mixed up with Ahyan's stuff.

I texted him and asked him to meet me near the storage room. Excitedly, he came downstairs but was soon disappointed that I had called him to look for the earring.

"*Arey*, I will get you a new one," he said tiredly. "Forget about that one."

"I cannot," I cried, sitting down on the floor where we fucked last night. "It was given to me by my brother, Ahyan."

"Good you got rid of it then," he commented bitterly as I shook my head in disapproval.

"Okay, sorry," he apologized instantly. "We will find this thing; I will look through my laundry and stuff."

"Thank you," I heaved a sigh of relief.

"But what will I get in return?"

"What do you want?" I asked and then said, "No…" He made a dirty face. "I won't blow you."

"Then forget the earring," he said like a bratty princess.

"I fucking hate you…" I got up and decided to leave as my mother had given me loads of work.

"Where are you going?" he was shocked as if I was doing something wrong.

"Going out," I replied casually. "Mother has asked me to do some stuff…"

"But…." he looked dismayed and hurt, "without giving me anything…"

"What do you want?" I growled standing by the door. I failed to understand Ahyan sometimes. Actually, I failed to understand him most of the days.

"Oh come on," he tried to pull me closer but I jerked back. "Ria?"

"Ahyan, we are playing with fire here," I said seriously and he again got mad. "We can't do this again and again. I have already been caught once. We gotta play safe."

"We are safe here," he whined miserably. Boy, the things men do for sex.

"No, we are not and I'm not arguing on this," I replied and opened the door to find few cows outside.

"At least a kiss?" he said in a sweet voice, looking harmless.

"Okay." Before I could say the next word, I was pushed against the wall. We kissed for a while after which I could not breathe so he shifted his attention to my neck, groping my ass.

Finally, when he stopped, there were no cows in sight, just my brother, Adi, watching us. I gasped, looking down as the saliva dribbled down my neck.

The next thing I felt was not Ahyan's tongue—which was a blessing, I realized then—but slaps.

My left cheek had turned redder than a porn star's ass and my nose was almost bleeding. Everyone was snarling at us, even people who didn't know who we were.

"This is the same guy, right?" asked Aditya as his wife and infant child stared at me, but with care and concern.

I looked at Ahyan who was sitting on the other end with his family. His father had punched him in the left eye and he could barely open it.

"Yes," I said clearly, suddenly not afraid of anything.

"I can't believe this girl! She has put shame…" my mother started her rants while my father sat disappointed next to Ahyan's father.

I kept my eyes lowered, numb. Not sure what was I supposed to do. Was I supposed to fight for us? I was a 26-year-old woman; I knew what I was doing. Neither of us had ever lied to each other. We both knew what we were doing. This was my life, my decision, my body. I would do what I wanted.

Everyone in the room was staring daggers at us with a filthy look in their eyes. As if they had never fucked before. The blood started dripping down my mouth as my mother continued venting.

"What should we do?" asked Ahyan's father to my uncle. He was sitting alone in a corner, tensed, because his son's wedding had turned more dramatic than he had anticipated.

"I cannot ask you to leave, Irfan," my uncle said looking at Ahyan's father with disappointment. "And I cannot ask my sister to leave either. You both are important to me."

"Then?" squealed my mother agitated by her own brother.

"If anyone should leave, it should be these two," he said snidely.

"What?" yelled my mother. "I cannot leave her anywhere alone, especially with him gone too."

I shook my head and looked down at the floor where my tears were falling.

"I think we should send them somewhere," my uncle suggested calmly. "Of course, separately, after what we hear they were doing…"

I looked up at Ahyan fearlessly and found him watching me. We knew we hadn't done anything wrong.

Chapter Three

Meera convinced my mother that she was on her side and made me stay with her in her room. My mother instructed her that under no circumstances was I to see Ahyan.

That night, we got horrible news that Mumbai, Bangalore, Paris, London, and Germany were under terrorists attack. Everything was shut down and the government imposed a strict curfew for two days.

When everyone had gone to bed, Ahyan sneaked in Meera's room to meet me. I was sitting in the balcony unaware of the time. He entered the room, his eye swollen, and hugged me tightly.

"How are you?" Looking at my face, he appeared sadder than my brother should have been after striking me. My nose had stopped bleeding but my cheek still burnt.

"Great," I smiled and he sat on the same chair beside me. "How is your eye?"

"I'm looking at you with one eye," he said and we laughed.

"Maybe you could get that pirate eye patch," I suggested leaning my head against his chest. "I always wanted to do a pirate."

"*Achha*," he laughed running his hands over my hair. "What are we going to do?"

We looked at each other with tears in our eyes.

"Fight," I replied pensively. "We must fight, Ahyan."

"But for what?" he asked, his hands still in my hair. I could hear his heartbeat.

"Everyone fights for love," I said staring blankly at the door. "We will fight for lust."

He didn't say anything and held my face in his hands and kissed my bruises. Smiling, I too kissed his eye gently and hugged him.

Since Sahil and Meera's wedding was postponed, we had two extra days to prepare. Everyone was either watching the news or staring at us weirdly. We felt worse than a terrorist probably would.

Somehow my mother came to know Ahyan and I secretly met in Meera's room. She could not be mad at the bride so she had me shifted back to my room where Veera and my sister-in-law, Bhumi, were to keep an eye on me.

In the afternoon, my brother and mother stormed inside the room staring madly at me.

"Now what did she do?" asked Veera, tired of being my babysitter.

"I checked your phone," my brother began, sitting on the stool while Bhumi fed my nephew, Palash.

"So?" I asked bored. "What's new in that?"

My mother was shocked that I had the balls to answer back my big brother.

"What is this?" he hissed flashing the phone in front of my face as I stared at my pictures Ahyan had clicked of me in the *burqa*.

"He is turning you, isn't he?" Aditya asked angrily while my mother had already started crying. Bhumi was consoling her as well as feeding the baby.

"He is not doing anything," I hissed back. "I asked him to get me a *burqa*. It was I who always wanted to wear it."

"Just like you wanted to read this," he said removing something from a thick jute bag. It was my book; it was the Quran I had borrowed from my friend, Nazni.

"How dare you go through my stuff?" I barked angrily, trying to snatch the book.

"What?" My mother's tears stopped as suddenly as they had started. "She is reading their books? She never read Gita when I offered her and now she is… *Hey bhagwan*…!!"

"Give me my book back," I stood in front of my brother fearless as he glared at me.

"Never," he sneered. "I will burn this before I give it to you."

"If you burn this," I gritted my teeth, "I will forget you are my brother and burn you with it."

"What?" my mother muttered crying again, "What are you saying, Ria? All this for that useless Muslim boy!?"

"Shut up!" I screamed. "He is not useless and stop obsessing over his religion. He is proud of it, I'm proud of it and so are many others."

"Well, so are the terrorists who are bombing our stations and hotels right now," commented my brother.

"Don't bring that shit into this," I shook my head at him. "You are better than this, Aditya. This is not what dad taught us."

"But you can't overlook that fact…"

"So you mean to say that Ahyan and every Muslim is a terrorist?" I yelled, frightening everyone in the room.

"I just want to know," my brother looked scared of me yet continued to yell, "if he is turning you into one of them?"

"No," I replied calmly, "he isn't. We don't talk about religion."

"Of course. You'd talk if you two could get time from keeping hands off each other!" he snarled and removed something from his pocket. It was my lost earring. "Found it on his bed and that's when I realized that my sister is up to something again. When I came down looking for her, well, the boy's hands were everywhere on her."

"Enough, Adi," said Bhumi, disgusted by whom, I had no idea.

"I don't care what you think of me," I said and snatched the Quran from of his hand. "Leave me alone."

Aditya left angrily while my mother stayed to torture me mentally. After an hour, which felt like an eternity, she left because my aunt had called her.

"Whatever you are doing is wrong," Veera said right after Bhumi left, leaving a sleeping Palash in bed.

"You should be the last person to lecture me, Veera," I sneered and saw Anushka and Sonam entering the room.

"Remember, lust is temporary," she pointed with her big snake-like eyes poking me.

"Then maybe," I turned around to face her, "I want to enjoy temporary things in life."

"You are just not getting it, Ria," she chided seeming to care. She only wanted to poke me, make me feel small in front of her.

"Do you wish to marry this guy?" she started throwing questions at me as she knew I could not get out of the room.

"None of your business," I muttered and Anushka passed me a sympathetic look.

"Do you even know his bank balance?" came another question. "What he does? Where does he work? How will he keep you if you two decide to marry, ever?"

"I don't know anything!" I screamed and got scared by my own voice. Thankfully, Palash didn't wake up and was busy dreaming something pleasant, hopefully.

"What is his salary, Ria?" she asked as everyone knew her *engineer husband* earned more than anyone in the family.

"I don't know." Shrugging I leaned forward, "I do know his dick's size. I suppose you don't wanna know that?"

Veera got so disgusted by me that she left the room immediately.

Next day, the situation had somewhat cooled down and things were getting back to normal in the world. But with my life, the terror had just begun.

Ahyan left a message through Sahil that he wanted to meet me and talk. I too wanted to talk to him but there was no way I could meet so easily now. I had eyes on me.

During noon, somehow, I managed to lie to Bhumi and ran down to the storage room. He was standing near the well. Before we could even hold hands my brother came down yelling my name.

Grabbing my hair, he pulled me inside the house. This angered

Ahyan and Sahil too, who pulled him away from me. Sahil held me while Ahyan pushed Aditya. Before Aditya could hit him, Ahyan's uncles came down.

It was decided that a decision had to be made about our situation. Only the people from our family were present in the hall, whereas Meera's relatives were sent to the other villa.

"I think we should get them married," suggested my father and my mother almost got a heart attack.

"It's not that easy, Akshay," my uncle said to my father. "I mean… what do you say, Irfan?"

Ahyan's father too agreed that it wasn't that easy to get us married.

"Then what do we do?" asked my father helplessly looking at me and then at the floor in disappointment.

"I think getting them married is the only solution," said Ahyan's uncle, Akram. "Then we won't have to keep them away from each other. We won't have to worry where they are and what they are doing."

"But…" stammered Ahyan and everyone silenced him. I looked at him with tears in my eyes.

"We can do it tomorrow itself," suggested my uncle, "along with Sahil and Meera."

"What is the matter with you, brother," shrieked my mother. "I'm not letting her marry him."

"Then what do you want?" screamed my father angrily.

"I think we should ask them what they want," suggested my aunt and now all the eyes were on us.

I took in a deep breath and spoke before Ahyan, "We have to say something…"

"Yes," nodded Ahyan. "We don't wanna get married."

I think my mother was the happiest in the room and almost jumped with joy upon hearing those words coming from her daughter's mouth.

"Then what do you two want?" barked my brother. "Fuck each other without marriage?"

"Yes," I commented and he almost got up to beat me. "Oh, sit down. Everyone in this room knows how many women you have fucked before marriage. So, sit down."

I felt bad, not because I spoke so ill about my brother but I had said so in front of Bhumi. But she knew what my brother was.

"Mind your language, you two," bellowed my mother while the so-called *sanskari* people looked at Aditya and me with disgust.

"There is no way you two can continue meeting without marriage," spoke Ahyan's uncle calmly to us. "Get this thing in your head."

"As if you will let us marry," said Ahyan daringly. "I know you won't. You never will because—" casting his eyes down, he paused. "This is one of the reasons why we both," he gave me a quick look, "promised each other that we won't fall in love."

"You two are going to stop this nonsense right now," snarled his father with fire in his eyes, "or else…"

"Or else what?" Ahyan asked with tears in his eyes. "You'll kill us both?"

"Nobody is killing anybody," my uncle said intervening. "Irfan, they are kids. They are immature. It happens."

"Well, the things they have done are not what kids do," his father commented and my mother agreed, nodding her head.

"How could you two even think of doing such a horrible thing? I never knew Ria, you would go to this extent and shame me like this. All the freedom I gave you…"

"Oh, shut up," I stopped my mother. "We just had sex. We have not committed any crime. I'm sure everyone in this room had sex at some point in time. With marriage, without marriage." I looked at Veera pointedly, "Even after marriage with someone else."

"Do you see how she is talking?" my mother said to everyone present in the room like it was a fucking court drama.

"I think we should send these two somewhere," my uncle spoke unexpectedly. "Irfan, you send Ahyan to someplace far away and Nita," he turned to my mother, "you send Ria someplace far away. I don't want them at my son's wedding. They have already ruined things."

"Who are you to say this?" said a startling voice. Sahil was watching his father curiously.

"What?" mouthed my uncle.

"This is my wedding," Sahil said angrily. "I'm the one who decides who gets to stay and who doesn't. I want both Ahyan and Ria at my wedding tomorrow or I'm not getting married."

Everyone looked at Meera expecting her to disagree with him but she sat there giving challenging looks to her future in-laws.

At last, it was decided that we were to attend the wedding the next day. But our destiny was to be decided after Sahil's wedding. I knew what was coming. Doom.

At around 4:30 am, I somehow managed to meet Ahyan with the help of Sahil and Meera.

We sat at the very place where everyone had ripped our dignity, self-esteem and poise to shreds earlier.

"What are we going to do tomorrow?" I was crying, my eyes swelling badly.

"I wish I knew, baby," he consoled me time and again, but my tears did not stop.

"How about we run away?" I suggested wiping my tears and gazing at him with hope.

"What?" Shock marred his beautiful face. "Where are we going to run to, Ria? And what are we going to do?"

"I don't know but I can't stay here, Ahyan," I begged him taking his hand in mine. "These people will get me married to some good for nothing dick or will torture me forever."

"But Ria..." before he could conclude his sentence Sahil came running.

"Ahyan's uncle's coming down, *quick!*" he told us to get up. "You two must leave now!"

"But I wanna talk to him, Sahil." I was crying like a baby.

"Not now, Ria," he pulled me up. "Tomorrow, at the wedding, you two can have plenty of time."

"But..." I tried to reach out to Ahyan but Sahil had taken me away from him.

9 hours later

Sahil was getting married and I was looking for Ahyan everywhere. My insides were churning, thinking what if he took off without saying goodbye or was sent away somewhere. I could not bear the thought of not seeing him, not touching him. I was burning in the fire ignited by both of us.

After the main ceremony, I spotted him with his father and was relieved. Grabbing him by his hand as soon I got a chance I took him to the backyard of the hall.

"We have to go, Ahyan," I suggested confidently because I could not think of anything else. "We cannot stay here. If we stay here, these people will ruin our lives."

"I cannot leave my family, Ria," he replied with an apologetic face. "I know they are angry but everything will cool down. Running away is not the solution. We don't even love each other. What are we going to do? Marry each other without love?"

"I'm not telling you to marry me, I'm just telling you to take me somewhere," I cried, my sobs growing louder. "We can go away from these people. They are not going to forgive us. There is no point in being patient. Trust me, we have to go."

"I cannot leave them." He looked dejected. "I just cannot do it."

"Ahyan, you have no idea what these people will do," I continued sobbing. "They will get me married in a week. Last time they threatened me but this time they will actually do it. Last time you chickened out, so you don't know what I went through. How I suffered!"

"Ria…" he whispered with tears in his eyes.

"I'm not being impulsive; last time was a lesson to me. I'm not going to make the same mistake again. I cannot make the same mistake again. I'm sorry." I apologized, why, I didn't know.

"If you have faith in me," Ahyan held my hand, "you will stay here, with your parents, till we find some way. Everything will be okay, let's give it time."

"I don't think it's going to be fine. I'm not exaggerating. I'm not going to ruin my life again. I have learned from my mistake. I'm sorry, but I stand by my decision," I shut my eyes and let the tears out.

"Don't cry, Ria," he hugged me and I kissed him on his lips.

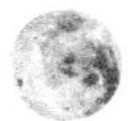

Clueless and betrayed I left packing my bags forever. In that moment, I didn't care about my parents or Ahyan. I only cared about my life. I don't know what happened afterwards. How my parents or Ahyan reacted? But as I sat in the train six hours later, my eyes closed to stop the tears, my mind kept running different scenarios. I had left him a letter. My only hope was for him to find it and let the words burn his soul. If he wouldn't come seeking me after reading the letter, I wished his heart burnt whenever he remembered my words.

I fell asleep and dreamt of Ahyan.

He finally understood I was nowhere to be seen.

He searched my room, his room, every single room but I was gone.

Dejected he went back to his room, thinking he had disappointed me. His eyes were filled with tears yet he saw the *burqa* lying on the bedside and a note beneath it.

Rubbing his eyes, he read it, fearing what I had done or was going to do.

I wrote this the first time I saw you walking in the college campus. Never got a chance to show you, but I'm sure you will like it:

I close my eyes, I open them. I close them, I open them. It's you everywhere. I cannot escape you. You are walking towards me like a gorgeous fantasy. That fuck-me face smiling, making my insides weak and vulnerable. My skin is hungry for your touch. I wish you were mine.

I don't know where I'm going, Ahyan. But I want you to find me (even if it's in death). Come and seek me. Look for me; don't give up on us so easily. Get up and fight for me. Fight for lust!

Part II

One year and few months later

Chapter Four

If you ask me to describe what I went through after I was betrayed, then I would like to quote something I read on the internet: *I would destroy you in the worst possible way and when I leave, you will finally understand why storms are named after people.*

Yes, I know why storms are named after people, but I'm still not sure who should I blame. Who destroyed me? He? Or I?

When someone breaks your heart you can at least mend it. It takes time, but you can mend it. But what do you do when someone breaks your spirit, your soul? What do you do when someone strips you of your dignity? I broke my rules for him, I changed myself for him, I fought with the world for him and he left me. Not once he thought about me when all I did was think about him, about us.

When all the drama was over. When he had left me, I thought everything was gonna be fine. I figured the worst was over; I was finally doing something good for myself. I thought it was the right thing to do. It's when you finally get yourself out of the mess and decide to do the right thing happiness comes easily to you. I was sure I was not gonna be that same girl, I was gonna be happy. But I waited for happiness, I waited and waited. Happiness too deceived me. In the end, even though I was doing the right thing, I was still unhappy. There was still a hole in my heart and nothing would ever fill that void. No matter what I did, I was still unhappy and lonely. So, what was the point of doing the right thing?

I never loved him neither did he love me. But it was so difficult to forget him, it was so difficult to accept the fact that he was not mine anymore, he was someone else's. Why was it so difficult? Why couldn't I understand something so simple? Why the heart still thought of him, even in the most perfect moments?

"Ria," I heard the familiar voice which greeted me every morning. It was soothing and caring.

"Ria, baby," the voice cooed, louder now, and I knew KJ was in my room waking me up. "Its 8, Ria."

Oh god, why did you make mornings? I rolled in my bed not wanting to leave it as I heard KJ shouting at his brother. "Param, get up, will you?"

KJ, full name Kawal Jeet, and Param were my roommates, more like my landlords. I was living with them for a year or so. When I landed in Shimla about a year back, I had no one to call my own and then one day I met KJ.

KJ was a widower who had lost his wife 10 years back in a car accident. After his wife's death, he didn't marry again as he believed no one could take her place. Param was KJ's brother who was single and gay. Due to his sexual orientation people weren't ready to accept him, except KJ. Their parents were alive but had abandoned Param.

KJ ran a small restaurant here in Shimla, whereas Param was a software engineer working at a local firm. After much struggle, I too managed to get a job at a primary school. The pay wasn't great but it was enough to survive, which was the need of the hour.

After a breakfast of toasts and boiled eggs we all left for our respective jobs. KJ and Param took the straight lane, whereas I, for a change, went through the tunnel.

I walked for some time and stopped in the middle of the road waiting for someone. I could see faint light at the end of the tunnel which meant he was here. He stood in front of me suddenly, removing the packet from his pocket, and eyeing me from top to bottom. Purab was my neighbour and my new supplier. He had the most haunting eyes and whenever I stared at them I wish I could write a poem dedicated to them.

"200 bucks," he muttered uninterested, his eyes and voice tired. I could see fresh wounds on his forehead where a few blotches of blood were shining.

"Here," I handed him the money and checked for the product as I hardly trusted a 20-year-old junkie.

"How come you are taking this from me?" he asked after I was done checking. "What happened to your usual supplier?"

"My supplier got arrested last week. You should know that," I stated the obvious. "You are in this business."

He pretended as if he didn't hear my words and nodded absently staring at the wall.

I knew it was time to move but I wanted to stay and talk more to him. I wanted to know the reason behind the most sorrowful eyes.

"Why are you doing this?" he asked before I could form a question to ask him.

"What?" I was taken aback.

"This," he repeated, staring at the packet still in my hand. "Why would a girl in her right mind want to do this? Why are you doing this?"

"Why do you do it?"I retorted and the colour from his face drained. He gave me a sad smile and shook his head, staring at his feet.

"Well, I will tell if you will tell me," I said wanting him to open up to me.

"Ahhh!" he laughed, showing a boyish grin and started kicking stones with his feet.

"Okay," I muttered and put the packet in my bag, getting ready to leave.

"It's because of a guy, isn't it?" he asked and my insides churned. I could not move for a few seconds. A guy. How did he know that? I tried not to show the disappointment on my face.

"It's getting late," I said, not meeting his eyes and walked away from him.

Param was very happy knowing that I had found a new supplier but KJ disapproved of our way of happiness.

"It's too risky," KJ shook head in displeasure. "First of all, he is our neighbour, plus how can you trust a 20-year-old kid?"

"Big deal, KJ," Param said shrugging and sniffing the joint. "He is easily accessible."

"But why do you two even have to take this bullshit?" questioned KJ as his long ponytail bounced up and down. KJ hated cutting his hair which resulted in a length which put my hair to shame.

"To get away from reality," muttered Param looking for a lighter in the basket near the TV as the doorbell rang.

"Wait. Don't light it," warned KJ as he got up to open the door. "This might be our new tenant."

KJ had another flat on the same floor, right opposite to ours. While he opened the door, I switched on the TV looking at Shahrukh and Kajol dance happily.

"Everything okay?" KJ asked our guest.

Param settled down beside me with a can of beer when I heard a familiar voice.

"Yes. Thank you."

My world stopped as I heard those words. Body in shock, I found it difficult to breathe and move. Param noticed my uneasiness and started rubbing my back. "You okay?"

When I looked at Param's face I had tears swimming in my eyes. He was confused by my reaction and kept asking me what had happened.

Standing up, I wiped the tears off my face and decided to face him. I didn't know if it was going to do me any good or not but I wanted to see his face.

Walking towards the door I could see KJ's back and his ponytail bouncing as he spoke gleefully to Ahyan. Param was staring at me in bewilderment.

"If you have any problem…" KJ was saying as I stood behind him. I stayed there gazing at the face which made my insides burn again with grief. Even though the face had not changed or aged, it didn't make any difference to me now. He glanced at me and diverted his attention back to KJ. *Wow*, he didn't recognize me. He didn't recognize the girl he broke and shattered miserably without a single thought. He didn't recognize her. *How wonderful*.

"So you have my number…" KJ said nodding his head and Ahyan looked at me again, his expression telling me that now he had recognized me. I turned and made my way to my room.

Param understood the reason for my tears was the man standing outside. Even though I had never shown them Ahyan's picture he realized it was the same Ahyan, *my* Ahyan.

"It's him, KJ," Param said for the hundredth time when we were having our dinner later.

"I'm sorry, baby," KJ assured me as I passed the *paratha* to him, not wanting to eat anymore. "If I had known I would have never even let him enter this building. In fact, I will return his deposit and throw him out."

"Yeah, throw the bastard out," muttered Param stuffing food in his mouth. "And for God's sake, Ria," passing me another *paratha*, he scolded, "eat! I don't want you to torture yourself because of some useless fuck."

"But I don't want to," I protested looking at my plate. "I might vomit…"

"Fine," Param said adamantly. "I will clean your puke. But eat."

"Yes, you people should eat," KJ said, cleaning his hands with the tissues lying on the table. "I will go talk to Ahyan."

"What, no!" I held on to his hand as he got up. "No, please. Don't kick him out. He will know why you are doing this and I don't want him to know that his presence still affects me."

"But it does, doesn't it?" protested Param dramatically.

"That's not important, Param," I replied crossly and looked at KJ with pleading eyes. "Please. Let him stay. How long did he say he is here for?" I asked looking down at my plate.

"For a month or so. He is here on a business trip." KJ added, "He is alone."

I closed my eyes so the tears could stop. He was alone, thank god.

Staring outside the window I pictured how different my life would have turned out if Ahyan would have never entered it. Would I have been this broken or sorted like all the girls I see on the streets every day? Would I have been one of those *normal* people whom I ran into every day? Ahyan put the abnormal in my life while he went back to live a normal one.

"Hey," I heard Param's voice as he entered my room in his grey-coloured pajamas. "Can't sleep?" he asked pulling a chair and joining me by the window.

"How can I?" I murmured still looking at the moon which was playing hide and seek with the clouds.

"Does it hurt?" Param asked after some time. "Seeing him again after such a long time?"

My eyes turned to Param's face which was probing me. "After this long, you don't feel anything."

"Well, I still get hurt when I see my ex-boyfriends posting pictures on Facebook," he laughed sadly. "But for you, it's the real deal. The shit is right in front of you."

"Yeah. I'm god's favorite," I shrugged smiling sadly. "He makes sure my shit's the real deal and it hurts the most."

"You must be so tired of this," he spoke unexpectedly, "After these many months you finally forgot this douche and then he appears again.."

"I knew," I whispered and yet Param heard, "we would meet again."

"Let KJ throw him out, Ria," Param moved his chair closer to mine. "It is so not worth it, hurting yourself all over again for some shitty piece of work."

"No," I said, holding up my tears. "Let him stay. Let's see how strong I am."

"You like this, don't you?" he asked amused, staring at me as the cold breeze entered the room, swinging my hair gently.

"What?" I asked suddenly, shining radiantly in the moonlight.

"Playing with your life," he said in the most non-offensive way. If it was someone else I might have thought the person was making fun of me or was ridiculing me but Param wasn't one of them.

"I want to sleep," I said, preferring not to answer.

"Okay," he watched me get up, understanding my silence more than my words. "Can I join you?"

"Of course," I jumped under the covers. I was used to Param sleeping with me. He often did it when he was heartbroken.

"Who broke your heart?" I asked when we were finally lying

beside each other.

"No one," he smiled and closed my eyes with his hands. "Sleep, honey."

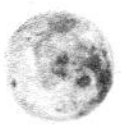

I knew Ahyan would find a way to talk to me as I was not making any efforts. The very next day he was waiting outside our door as I returned from school. I was carrying a bag full of groceries which almost slipped from my hands when I saw him smiling at me.

Unable to say anything I stood there transfixed, staring back at his beautiful face. He didn't know how to start the conversation after ruining my life so he kept smiling at me.

Finally, he understood that I was uncomfortable. "Ria," he said my name just like he used to, with passion and love. "I thought we should…" He came closer to me. My heart was in my mouth and I knew I was shaking with fear.

"Um, KJ is not at home," I uttered stupidly. "He will be home after 7 so why don't you come then."

"What?" he was perplexed but I kept on repeating the same thing.

"If you have any query regarding the house," I said finally opening the door as he blinked at me, confused, "I suggest you talk to KJ."

"But Ria, I want to…"

"He will be home after 7…" I repeated for the tenth time and stepped inside, banging the door on his face.

Breathing heavily, I felt stupid at first but then it made sense. Why should I talk to him when he failed to recognize me yesterday? What was he to me anymore?

"He had the balls to come and talk to you?" Param asked while we were dining. "How dare he!"

"What did he say?" KJ asked calmly while Param was still fuming.

"Nothing," I said stuffing my face with fried rice. "I didn't let him talk. Ran inside as soon as I could."

"Good," smiled Param while KJ asked him to shut up and eat.

"But you can't keep avoiding him forever," KJ made a point when my phone rang.

While I was checking the number which was unknown to me, Param started arguing why I could not keep avoiding Ahyan.

"Guys wait," I shushed them and answered the phone.

"Hey," came a boy's voice. "It's me, Purab."

"Who?" I asked as Param asked if it was Ahyan. I shook my head.

"Your supplier," he stated hesitantly.

"Oh, Purab," I yelled finally picturing the boy with baggy clothes. Both KJ and Param were staring at me in surprise.

"I needed a favour from you," he said and I bit my lip.

"What is it?" I asked despite wanting to disconnect the phone.

"Can I crash at your place for just one night?" he asked and my instant answer was no but before I could say so, he continued, "My mom kicked me out."

"Oh!" I gasped and nodded. "Fine. Where are you?"

"Outside the building."

I begged KJ to let him stay for a night, he agreed after much consideration. Param was excited to stay with our supplier. KJ told him that Purab was a drug supplier not Santa Claus with gifts.

He rang the bell few minutes later and waited meekly outside. Purab was dressed in a dark green t-shirt which complimented his fair complexion and loose blue jeans. He looked like a fragile boy standing outside his school.

"Come in," I smiled as KJ and Param stared at him.

"Thank you," he said smiling awkwardly. "Thanks a lot."

KJ nodded and went inside but Param kept stared at him, scanning him, especially his pockets. At first I thought he was hitting on the boy but then I realized he wanted a joint.

"So, um, you sleep here on the couch," I told him once Param and KJ were in their rooms. "Param will bring you a pillow and a blanket for the night. I hope that's okay?"

"Of course," he nodded. I stood there for a bit wondering if I should ask him why his mother kicked him out.

One look at those sad eyes made me want to cry. How much had he suffered already at such a young age?

"I will leave you then," I said and switched off the lights. I could still see those sad eyes staring at me.

Chapter Five

Next day, Purab left our apartment saying he was gonna crash at a friend's place for a few days. Without asking any questions I let him go. KJ preferred to stay quiet till Purab left, while Param had lost hope that the boy had any stash with him.

Thankfully, I didn't run into Ahyan in the morning and hoped that he won't bother me again. While returning home I prayed I won't run into him again. While I was busy planning my strategies to avoid him henceforth, I saw Purab walking with two men. By the looks of it, he was doing less of walking and more of being dragged away by those men. They were holding on to his arm forcefully.

I followed them and ended up in a deserted place where they started beating him up. I almost dropped my bag when I saw Purab was already bleeding from his lip. He was motionless, taking the trashing as it came. I panicked and could not see him being beaten to death.

Screaming, I told those two men to back off as I called the police on my phone. I knew it was an idiotic thing to do. They could have dragged me and beaten me too but I had to stop them from hitting Purab who seemed to have lost consciousness.

The men looked at me and then at the phone in my hand, and to my relief, ran away. I didn't know I had the balls to make two thugs disappear. They weren't heavy or beefy that it was impossible to defeat them but I was in no mood to wrestle.

I ran towards Purab and offered him some water from my bottle. He opened his eyes, his lip bleeding profusely. "Thanks again," he whispered.

"No problem," I offered him my handkerchief to stop his lip from bleeding.

"You think you can walk?" I asked worriedly when he got up and tried to sit straight.

We took a cab and reached home. Purab said his mother was out and hopefully won't see us together. I didn't care if anybody saw me with him.

I took him upstairs with his one hand around my shoulder and my hand around his waist to support him. On our floor, Ahyan was standing outside my door again. I froze and Purab understood something was wrong. But when Ahyan saw me with a guy, he looked unhappy. I was glad because I knew he won't try to talk to me in front of Purab.

Suddenly, Purab's hand slipped from my shoulders and reached my waist, which he grabbed tightly. Seeing this, Ahyan walked away from us. I opened the door and made him sit on the bed where he had slept last night.

"It's him, isn't he?" he asked gulping water while I brought some bandages to clean his wound. "The reason why you are like this."

Like this? What did 'like this' mean? Lost? Damaged? Fucked-up?

"How did you know?" I asked meeting his eyes.

"Your eyes," he said looking into them while I blinked. "They told me everything. The way you looked at him. It was like staring at a tragedy. Staring at the biggest mistake of your life. The wounded staring back at its torturer."

"You are smart," I said and headed off to my room to change my clothes which had Purab's blood on them.

I locked the door and changed into my pajamas which Param had bought for me last month. When I returned, I saw another lost soul sitting alone, basking in his melancholy.

"Can I get something to eat?" he asked, pressing the cotton against his lip.

"Okay, give me five minutes," I told him and he smiled at me, his eyes twinkling.

I made him a simple sandwich and dropped the plate on his lap. He devoured the sandwich as if he had not eaten in years.

"Thinking about him?" Purab asked as I was trying to erase Ahyan's face from my memories.

"What did he do?" Purab shot another question. "I mean, you can share if you want to…"

"He left me," I said and took a bite of his sandwich.

"And now he is back," he said the dreadful words slowly.

"Not for me," I whispered more to myself.

"Will you forgive him?" he asked and I regretted helping him and offering him a sandwich.

"Huh?" I frowned.

"It's clear that he is here to apologize," he stated, finishing the sandwich. "Must have been standing here for a while and was clearly pissed seeing you with some other guy."

I raised my eyebrows, "Is that why you grabbed my waist?"

"Yes," he smiled.

"Nothing matters now," I said tiredly. "He is married."

"It does not matter to us," Purab said and I rolled my eyes.

"Will you forgive him?" he asked again and I emitted fire from my eyes. "Got it."

"Who were those guys beating you up, smarty?" I questioned and could see him getting a little annoyed.

"You won't answer my question," he said putting the plate aside, "I won't answer yours. Anyway, thanks again for helping me."

"No problem," I nodded and got up. "Lock the door behind you and leave."

With those words, I left him alone as I made my way to my room, wanting to cry.

Ahyan tried to talk to me a few times even after that but I was in no mood to listen to his lies and false promises. I thought I've had enough.

One night he barged into our house like a mad hound and started looking for me everywhere. I was in my room and after hearing his voice I decided to stay there for as long as I could. KJ reasoned with him and asked him humbly to get the fuck out of the house.

"I need to talk to her just once," he kept repeating the same line while I listened to every word through the door.

"She does not want to talk to you," I heard Param raise his voice. Param never spoke to anyone like that, not even his enemies. Something was wrong with him.

"Please KJ," Ahyan was begging, "Tell her to talk to me once. It's killing me."

"It should," KJ replied calmly. "If she could try to end her life for you then something should kill you too."

"What?" Ahyan sounded aghast. "She tried to kill herself?"

I closed my eyes as tears fell slowly down my cheeks. KJ and Param were not just my landlord/roomies but two people who saved me when I tried to jump off the bridge on Ahyan's wedding day. They not only saved me but brought me home and made me somewhat normal. At least I never tried to kill myself after that day.

"I think you should leave." I heard the door opening and closing after that. No words. No arguments. No pleading.

The next day Ahyan was waiting for me outside my school, still wearing previous day's clothes. His hair said it had not been combed for days. His grey t-shirt was hanging loosely from his body. Stubble on his gorgeous face was growing thick. But what attracted me the most were his eyes. I stared at them and realized for the first time that they didn't talk to me. I could easily read Param's eyes, or KJ's when he missed his wife. Hell, I could stare in Purab's eyes and read a thousand tales but Ahyan had the most amazing eyes. They never spoke to anyone. They hid his secrets well and intact. How did he do it? How could he hide his agony, pain, emotions so easily?

I looked away from his dead eyes and started walking. He stalked me and begged me to stop.

"Please, stop," he said matching steps with mine. "I need to talk just once, Ria, *please*," he screamed the last two words grabbing my arm.

"Don't touch me," I pushed him so hard that he almost lost his balance. We had reached the tunnel where I had bought pot from Purab a few days back. It was again deserted except for a few crows.

"What do you want to talk about?" I screamed as he looked at me intently.

"Did you end your marriage?" I asked and could see the discomfort on his face. "Or bored of fucking your wife and need something new?"

"I just need to talk," he said trying to sound polite but I could see his anger was quite close to the surface.

"What do you want to talk about, Ahyan?" I shouted once again which startled him. "What's left to talk? I'm sure you are not here to apologize to me."

"I did ask you not to take any hasty decision," he began mumbling something which I had no intention of listening. I turned to walk home, but he pulled on my arm and dragged me inside the tunnel.

"Let me go!" I tried to break his grip but he was strong. "What are you doing?"

"Talking to you," he said finally letting my arm go. "Your bodyguards don't let me come anywhere near you." He paused. "Is it true, Ria?" I looked up at his face. "Did you try to kill yourself?"

"I'm leaving." I pushed him away but he grabbed my hands and pinned me against the wall. "Ahyan…"

"You really tried to kill yourself?" he asked softly, our eyes locked with each other's.

I didn't want to answer him so I stayed silent.

"Please, Ria," he begged, his face a picture of innocence. "Tell me what happened."

"You really wanna know what happened?" I asked crying. "You really wanna know what happened, you asshole!" I cried and pushed him back.

"Here's what happened," wiping the tears off, I spoke, "You left me, Ahyan. That's what happened. You left me stranded all alone on a deserted road."

His eyes looked at me blankly, no hint of remorse in them.

"Did you try to find out what happened to the girl you left behind? Do you know what happened to the girl who left everything for you? Do you know under what circumstances she lived? She was cheated, betrayed by you, humiliated in front of the whole family, disgraced for life, lost her self-respect, was lonely when you were enjoying your wedding, smiling, laughing, welcoming your new life."

His eyes were moist now.

"You were already engaged when you met me at my brother's wedding." I was unable to stop my tears, my grief pouring out of me openly. He looked dumbstruck. "Yes, Ahyan, I know the actual truth why your father never wanted us to marry even though your uncle suggested it. You were already engaged to your now wife and yet every minute we spent together, you didn't bother to mention that even once."

"I was never happy with that relationship; it was forced on me…" He finally opened his mouth.

"I don't care," I wanted to scream at him but I felt exhausted. "It was your fucking problem. Why did you fuck my life for that? You should have had the fucking balls to stand up and talk to your family but you never had and you never will."

"You betrayed me, Ahyan," I breathed, shaking my head. "You didn't even bother to lie to me; just hid the truth from me which tells me only one thing—that I wasn't even worth knowing the truth. If I was important to you, you would have told me the truth or bothered to lie but you hid everything from me which shows what I was to you."

"I was lost, Ria," he said in a remorseful voice.

"The day you got married," I remembered the horrific day when I realized I was so weak, "I stood at the edge of the bridge and decided to jump. But before I jumped I wished only unhappiness to you. Wished for you to rot in your own grief." Staring at his stunned face I smiled sadly. "I wished you were dead, not married. I thought, at least if you were dead, I would remember you fondly but no, you got married, and I only cursed and cursed and cursed you after that."

"You must be very happy to see me this distressed then?" he asked, angry now. His face and voice changed, like a chameleon. He glared at me waiting for my answer.

"I should be but I don't give a fuck anymore." I turned and walked away from him. It was true; Ahyan was more or less dead to me.

Chapter Six

Ahyan didn't bother me for a few days after the verbal bashing in the tunnel. I knew this would happen. My wish for him to be unhappy must have hurt his ego and balls.

Param's birthday was here and we decided to celebrate it, but he said he already had plans with someone special. His someone special changed every month since they dumped him easily. But this time he was sure that the new guy was 'the one'. But Param came home crying that night as his *someone special* had stood him up.

"Always," KJ said angrily. "Always these men make a fool of this guy!"

"Please KJ," I tried to calm him down as Param cried, hugging me. "Don't shout at him right now. It's not the time."

"Then when is the right time, Ria?" He was now furious with me. Tired of venting, he went to his room, slamming the door behind him.

I suggested we do something so Param could forget this never-ending agony. He wanted just one thing and I decided to give him that.

I called Purab and asked him to deliver a few joints. I knew he would not refuse me at any cost after what I had done for him. He rang the bell some 45 minutes later and KJ was even more frustrated to see the junkie back in the house. Param wanted Purab to stay and *celebrate* his birthday properly. KJ joined us initially but called it a night soon after, keeping few *parathas* for us on the table. I think we smoked for a long time that night.

Next morning brought many surprises. I was in my bed, my throat dry as my sex life. But there was something unusual about this morning. Everything felt soft and smooth beneath my skin. It was only after I opened my eyes I realized I was naked and not alone in bed.

Instantly, I got up and noticed someone was snoring beside me. There was no way I had slept naked with Param in the same bed.

Carefully, I pushed the blanket off the person's face and saw Purab smiling innocently in his sleep. I shook him hard and asked him to get up. He started yelling in his half-asleep state, shocked upon finding me in front of him.

I shook him again as he wasn't entirely awake yet and most of his blanket slipped away, revealing him to be naked as well.

Fuck! I slept with a boy. I slept with a junkie. There is a naked junkie in my bed! These thoughts started stabbing my head as I tried hard to remember what actually we had done last night.

"Purab!" I screamed and he jumped up in bed immediately.

"Good morning," he smiled and realized quickly that something was wrong.

Running his eyes under the blanket he became aware of his nakedness. His eyes moved to me, not my face, my naked body which was hidden under the white sheet. It annoyed me that he could not look away.

"What the fuck are you looking at?" I snapped my fingers in front of his dreamy eyes.

"I'm sorry," he looked down shaking his head, "I was just trying to remember…"

"So, um, even you don't remember what happened last night?" I was annoyed and horrified. He shook his head.

"Maybe we didn't do anything…" he suggested dumbly.

"Then why the hell are you in my bed naked?" I said as he scratched his head pretending to think hard.

"I don't even remember smoking pot with you," he mumbled as I racked my brain to remember at least one tiny detail.

Then we heard another voice from under the bed. Something slammed against the frame and finally came out. Param.

"Hey," he smiled standing up, taking his time. "Oh god!" he gasped looking at our heap of clothes on the floor.

"Ria!" he screeched. "Did you fuck him?"

"No," I answered automatically with an embarrassed face.

"We don't remember," came from the naked junkie.

"Wow!" exclaimed Param sitting on the edge of the bed. "You finally get laid after such a long time and you don't even remember it. Simply wow."

"I was thinking…maybe we didn't do it?" suggested Purab again and Param made an are-you-fucking-kidding-me face at him.

"Dude, you are naked," he eyed Purab and then me, "with a very hot woman in the same bed and you say you didn't do anything? Then it's your loss." Laughing, he raised his hand for a high-five but I shook my head in dismay.

"Do you remember anything?" Purab asked Param avoiding my sorrowful face. "How did we end up here?"

"Oh, I remember," Param said thinking hard. "Ria insisted that we come to her room as she wanted to show us something."

"What?" asked Purab, hoping it would make sense.

"I don't remember that," Param shrugged and then winked at him. "Maybe something she showed *you* afterward."

"Param," I chided, glaring at him. "So that's the only thing you remember? My suggesting we all come in here?"

"Yup," nodded Param. "Then I think I passed out or something… but don't remember how I got under the bed." I was disappointed only to be jolted back to reality when Param screamed, *Oh my god!* This means you guys fucked while I was under the bed."

It was quite an obvious thing and yet it took so much time for us to figure out.

"Oh!" Purab made an interesting noise.

"Oh no," I whispered and Purab understood I was upset.

He looked at me expecting me to say something but I was finding it difficult to use words.

He finally gathered up some courage and clearing his throat awkwardly, said, "Ria, maybe we just got naked and slept. It's a possibility that we didn't do anything."

Param passed me a look, giggling and nodding his head vigorously, wanting to believe Purab's version but he just could not.

"Maybe," I said loudly more to myself than anyone else. "Yes, maybe we just slept…"

Purab forced a smile and looked at me differently. His eyes were talking to me; they wanted to come near me. I had a flash of a memory and instantly looked down at my nails.

Fuck! My left middle finger's nail was broken unevenly. I looked up confused and asked Purab to turn around. Param got excited and jumped up from the bed.

Few long scratches covered his back, still pink and raw. And we now knew what had happened. We *had* fucked last night with Param sleeping under the bed.

I ran my fingers over the red marks and Purab danced with my single touch. Param went out of the room, screaming in joy that I finally got laid.

KJ walked in wearing the usual apron with a pan in his hand. "What's the matter?"

"They did it last night," Param jumped like a little child, "while I was under the bed."

"*Cheee!*" KJ made a disgusting face which made me feel even more nasty.

"We didn't do it on purpose," Purab tried defending us which made me melt a little.

"Oh my god," I suddenly grabbed the white sheet to cover me entirely.

"What? What now?" asked Param excitedly. "Did you remember something?"

"No," I shook my head getting out of bed. "But I'm sure if we don't remember this, then we didn't even remember to use a condom…" I pushed Param out of the way.

"Where are you going?" Param came after me as I ran to the washroom. "To buy a condom now?" He sounded a little too gleeful.

"Shut up, Param," I muttered from inside. "Get me something to wear, please. I need to buy a morning-after pill."

"So," KJ said as Purab gathered his clothes, "how old are you? Please don't tell me you are underage."

"No," Purab replied as he quickly put on his clothes shamelessly in front of KJ. "I'm 20."

KJ diverted his eyes, fixing them on one of our neighbours out on her balcony. "Definitely a virgin."

"No," Purab answered smugly as Param joined them, "Lost it when I was 18."

"Cool," Param was impressed and winked at his older brother which made KJ mad.

"Anyway, tell her that I'm leaving," Purab said meekly to Param, "and if there is anything she needs, call me."

"Oh, she will call you for sure, honey," Param teased as KJ taunted him about his 100th breakup.

It had been three days and nobody had seen Ahyan get out of the house. KJ feared he had killed himself but I knew Ahyan didn't have the balls to harm himself. For some reason, KJ was worried and Param was indifferent.

One chilly day KJ returned home early from the shop and knocked on Ahyan's door. But no one answered.

"We have to do something," KJ pleaded to me. I nodded.

"Call the police," Param said ruthlessly. "They will clean the mess."

"What if he is alive?" asked KJ and it gave me a little relief which also made me feel sick.

"He might be," murmured Param getting up from the chair and heading towards the kitchen. "It's my turn to cook so I'll see you guys later."

KJ stared at me not knowing what to say.

"Do you want *bhindi* or *aloo* tonight?" Param yelled from inside the kitchen.

"I think *you* should knock on the door," suggested KJ while I stared at him in horror.

"Guys?" Param yelled again as I bit my lip making the decision. "*Fine*, both it is."

"Try calling him out by saying his name," KJ said slowly. "I have a feeling he will open the door."

"Okay," I whimpered.

Standing outside Ahyan's door was so hard. I could not knock on it; it felt like knocking on the door to my past. But I needed to know if he was alive or not. A tiny knock. No answer.

I knocked again and still no answer. Why was he doing this? What had he done to himself?

Tears pooled in my eyes thinking of everything we had done together and where we were standing presently.

"Ahyan," I said loudly, my voice quivering due to tears. "Ahyan?"

Immediately, I heard a commotion inside and the door slowly opened. There was no one standing by the door, it opened like it happens in horror movies. Looking back at KJ, I asked what was I supposed to do. He signalled me to get in. Hesitantly, I moved my feet forward.

The room smelled like Ahyan—the first time I had touched him and the smell of him from the time we made out, it was the same smell. As the room was dimly lit I could hardly see him but as soon as he slammed the door shut I knew he was standing behind it.

"Switch on the lights," I said putting some authority behind my voice and he obeyed me immediately, something which even in that bizarre situation surprised me.

He had grown a beard and looked like a boy who was going through a college break-up.

We heard KJ's frantic voice from outside as he thought Ahyan might hurt me in some way. I assured him that nothing was wrong and I would be out after talking to him.

"What do you wanna talk about?" he asked sitting on a sofa which was crumpled beyond recognition. It seemed he had been lying dead on it these past few days.

"What have you been doing?" I asked uninterested. "KJ was worried about you."

"Look at you," he sneered at me while I frowned at him. "Not a tiny fiber inside you is worried about me and I can sense it from your tone. You are just worried I would spread shit in your friend's apartment. Don't worry; I won't die here even if I desire so."

"What the fuck has happened to you, Ahyan?" I asked suddenly terrified of this man.

"Life," he murmured and gulped down water from a plastic bottle. Then I noticed it was not water, it was alcohol. Ahyan was drinking alcohol; the man who despised it and wanted to ban it all over the world was now consuming alcohol.

"Is that alcohol?" I asked still staring at the bottle as he looked up at me and nodded.

"You must be so happy to see me like this," he chuckled as I could not open my mouth to defend myself.

Ideally, I should have been happy to see him suffer so much. I should have been celebrating but I just stood there gazing at him thinking what on earth went wrong with him. I thought I was the fucked-up one but even here Ahyan stole my thunder. Was he more fucked-up than me? Then I glanced at his face, tipsy Ahyan struggling to even get up. Oh, he was much more fucked-up than I ever was. And he was alone here. I still had Param, KJ and maybe Purab, but Ahyan had no one.

"Wasn't this something you wanted to see happen?" he asked, somehow getting up and interrupting my thoughts. My insides were screaming with a loud *yes*.

"I don't give a fuck," I gritted my teeth angrily and made my way to the door but he held my wrist.

"No, wait," he hissed, his mouth smelling of vodka. "Answer me first. How happy are you to see me like this? Does the thought of me in such a pathetic state give you an orgasm?"

I preferred not to answer and gazed into those beautiful eyes which seemed haunted. What the fuck happened to us? What had we done to each other?

"Answer me, you bitch!" he yelled and the word *bitch* brought me back to reality. This was the same Ahyan I had left years back, but a bit more fucked-up. Old habits never die, some say. Ahyan's old habit of calling me a bitch whenever he was mad never died either. But why was he calling me a bitch now? He had a wife. Maybe he was tired of abusing her.

I found my voice and answered, "Don't you dare call me a bitch, you fucking slut."

It angered him more and he pinned my arms against the wall aggressively. *"What!?"*

"You heard me, Ahyan," I hissed struggling to fight back and get away from the monster.

"You dare answer me back," he laughed tightening his grip. "What, you don't want me anymore, huh?"

"What?" I looked him in the eye and he leaned in to kiss me. I was strong enough to kick him with my leg but he was stronger.

"Ahyan, stop it!" but he had gone deaf and was trying to grip my face with one of his hands. When he couldn't do that he moved his lips to my neck and I kicked his balls hard.

He instantly dropped to the floor, crying out in pain. That did satisfy me; the sight of him hurt and lying on the floor soothed my soul.

"This is what you deserve, Ahyan." I screamed, crying, "Unhappiness and pain. Yes, I love to see you like this. I love the fact that you are pathetic. I love watching you unhappy. In fact, I'm going to feed on your unhappiness. I never wanted to hurt anyone so much physically as well as mentally as I want to harm you, you fucking asshole."

He didn't move, not in rage or to even hit me. It made me realize my speech had gone in vain. Fuck, did I kill him?

I knelt beside him and felt his pulse. He was unconscious. Fucking moron kept asking me to answer and when I did, he had to pass out. I kicked his legs hard and walked out of the flat.

"It's been two days and you are still thinking about that asshole," ranted Param as I stared at the cheese pizza lying in front of me.

"No, I'm not," I replied and picked up a now cold slice.

"Oh dearie, you still are and I can see it," he commented gazing at me, possibly judging me.

"I just…" swallowing the words I looked down and shook my head. "I just…"

"What?" he asked irritated, hating the mere mention of Ahyan.

"I just… I always thought that he might be happy," I said after swallowing the stone-cold pizza. "I believed I was rotting here and he was happy but then I saw him that day," narrowing my eyes, I opened up my heart, "and he was so helpless and fucked-up, just like the way I wanted him to be." Param looked surprised. "In fact, he is more messed up than I ever imagined."

"So, isn't that good, Ria?" he spoke with a jubilant smile on his face as he dreamily looked up at me. "I wish I could see one of my ex-boyfriends so fucked-up."

"I don't know if it's good or not," I added. The doorbell rang, putting a stop to our conversation. "Who could it be?" I shifted my eyes to the clock on the wall. 9:30pm.

"Oh, it's a surprise for you." Param opened the door and I saw Purab in a loose black shirt and blue jeans.

"What is he doing here?" I asked rudely while he stood by the door.

"Oh, I invited him." Param signalled Purab to sit with us. "KJ is out so I thought we could have a party."

"Party?" I raised my eyebrow and Purab passed a huge bag to him.

"Alcohol," cheered Param happily stepping inside the kitchen to grab us glasses.

I was left alone with Purab which made me want to kill myself. The silence was making things even more uncomfortable. I looked at him and found him staring at me.

Annoyed, I said, "What?"

"Sorry," averting his gaze, he shook his head. "I'm so sorry…"

We started with white rum Purab had bought with Param's money. Param was already sloshed and singing Taylor Swift's songs. I could not believe I was sitting here and drinking with a boy I had accidentally slept with a few days ago. Thankfully, we still did not remember anything from that night.

As I poured myself another glass I was instantly reminded of the bottle I had seen at Ahyan's place. I put the glass down and shut my eyes throwing my head back.

"Are you okay?" I heard a voice. It wasn't Param as he was still singing something in a language nobody understood.

"I'm fine," I replied modestly to make up for my rudeness from earlier. He smiled at me.

"Are you drunk?" he asked scanning my face. I shook my head.

After a while, Param was close to passing out while I was sitting by the window staring outside at the street. It was deserted which meant that it had to be late in the night now. I noticed some movement and saw a lanky dude entering the building. My first thought was Ahyan. Rubbing my eyes I looked at him carefully but he was already gone.

I again closed my eyes and saw Ahyan's face; he looked beautiful, and not that pathetic drunk Ahyan. The handsome one, shaved, wearing a white *kurta* and smiling at someone, that someone being me in a beautiful *burqa*. We were near a mosque, happy, laughing as he said something funny only for my ears.

"Hey," I felt his hand on my shoulder. "Ria?"

"Ahyan," I whispered and felt someone shaking me lightly.

"Ria?" This voice was different. It wasn't that mesmerizing devil's voice but sounded like that of a boy.

"Ria? Are you okay?" Purab asked sitting beside me on the floor.

Opening my eyes I saw Purab's face. There was so much innocence in there. Smiling, I nodded my head.

"Yes, I'm fine," I said still smiling, suddenly finding Purab nice and comforting.

"Are you drunk?" he asked again and I laughed seeing Param lying on the floor snoring loudly.

"Yes," I frowned, "I think so…"

"Great," he murmured slowly. "I was thinking that, um, since we don't remember sleeping with each other, why don't we do it this time for real and remember it?"

"What? No," I laughed, trying to get up.

"But why?" he held my hand tightly. "Please, Ria. Since that night I can't stop thinking how it would have been. I can't stop thinking about you."

"Um," I stared at his face, it was miserable just like a puppy's. "I don't know…"

"Come on, please?" he begged.

"No," I said firmly and finally stood up. "Will you help me in getting Param up?"

After some time he replied, "Sure. Why not?"

We shifted Param from living room's floor and into his bed. Even though he was thin, he was heavy and it took a while for us to reach his room. We dumped him on the bed and Purab covered him with a blanket.

When we reached my room, he smiled and wished me good night. "Sleep well."

I didn't respond and stared at his dejected face as he reached the door.

"Purab," I called out to him biting my lip hard, "I was wondering if…"

"Yes?" he asked hopefully. His disappointment had drained away in an instant and he was waiting for me to say the golden words—'Fuck me'.

"Maybe you are right," I finally said it after a lot of thinking. "We should do it one more time. Just for the sake of remembering what really must have happened. Perhaps if we do it…" he smiled looking cheerful and almost ran towards me, "we might remember…" but he didn't let me finish the sentence and kissed me on my mouth fiercely. Thank god, I thought. I was talking bullshit anyway, just trying to get a teenage boy in my pants so desperately.

Opening the door, Purab led me inside, his lips still on mine. Soon we were on my bed as his hands moved all over my body.

"Hey," he whispered in my ears, "are you sure you are not so drunk that you will forget this night?"

"No," I shook my head smiling. "I won't forget it and even if I do, I suggest that you make it unforgettable." I winked.

He grinned moving his hands inside my t-shirt, "I will."

"Purab," I whispered as his cold hands cupped my breast, "Condom?"

"Oh." With his left hand he removed a pack from his back pocket. "Got it."

"Did you know we were gonna do it?" I asked startled and impressed.

"No," he shook head innocently. "Param asked me to bring it for him. Since he is asleep, I guess we can use them, right?"

Laughing, I kissed him. "Of course. And I think Param asked you to bring them for us."

But he wasn't listening to me anymore and his cold hands were tugging my pants down.

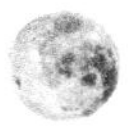

Opening my eyes, I felt darkness around me. Purab was lying by my side, sleeping innocently, naked. He looked so pure with his eyes closed.

Whenever Ahyan and I had sex it could only be described as fucking. A meaningless fuck. No one would call it making love. But with Purab it was making love; it was tender, meaningful and memorable.

Thinking that brought a smile to my face.

"What are you smiling at?" Purab said sleepily.

"Nothing."

I turned to his side and he pulled me closer to him. "It's still dark. Go back to sleep."

"Okay," I hugged him and closed my eyes. He was as thin as Ahyan but his hands and arms were comforting, not torturous or forceful.

It was a dreamless sleep and yet I felt I heard something. KJ must be home because it was still dark everywhere. There was no way Param would wake up so early.

Our door was slightly ajar and I knew KJ would start yelling once he saw that I was in bed with a boy. But there was no sound so I opened my eyes and found the last person I wanted to see standing there.

Ahyan looked at me as if I had betrayed him. Like I tore his heart and splashed it all over the room painting the walls with his blood. How could he look at me like that when he was the one who made me feel like that every day?

I was returning from school and was busy thinking about nothing as usual when all of a sudden felt someone's arm on my shoulder.

"Hey," said Purab panting and catching his breath. "I was screaming your name but you..." he found it difficult to talk, huffing, he shut his mouth for a while before flashing me his boyish grin. "Sorry. I ran really fast to catch you."

"That's okay," I smiled as a woman passed by giving us a look. Purab's hand was still on my shoulder.

"So can we walk?" I asked awkwardly. "We will go slower, for you."

"Of course," he took his hand off my shoulder. "After you."

"Where were you lost?" I didn't say anything and checked him out. He was in a dark blue t-shirt and black jeans with a backpack slung over his shoulder.

"Are you returning from college?" I asked and he smiled proudly at me.

"Oh my god," I almost screamed and thankfully there was no one around. "That is so great."

"Isn't it?" he asked smiling gleefully. "My mother's happy too. I have even started living with her again. She seems content."

"This *is* great," I said truly unable to stop smiling. "I'm happy too, Purab."

"You are?" he asked surprised, his face glowing. "That's worth it then."

"You should study properly," I began lecturing as we reached the tunnel where once we had exchanged the product.

"Come on," he said looking inside. "I need to show you something."

"What is it?" surprised, I asked, as no one was on the streets anyway. "Show me here…"

"Nah. Inside," he insisted and walked in. Few seconds later I followed him in. I could barely see anything and almost tripped but he held my hand.

Smiling, I thanked him and he kissed me on my mouth without my permission.

"What is this?" I asked pushing him away while he stared at me, appalled.

"I don't know," he shrugged not meeting my eyes. "I just wanted to kiss you, that's all."

"Um, Purab," I bit my lip and looked into his eyes. "We can't keep doing this forever…"

"Why not?" he protested so loudly that his voice echoed in the tunnel. "It makes both of us happy."

"Yes, but," I was finding it difficult to argue with a kid, "we don't know what we are. We must at least define what we are."

"Okay," he nodded, trying to look thoughtful but he was still a kid. "Whatever you say, but I can't afford to lose you."

"What?" I looked up startled. "Why? You can get plenty of girls your age just for sex…"

"It's not just sex, Ria." He suddenly sounded like a man. "You make me happy. The thought of meeting you makes me happy, it makes me wanna do things. I don't want to lose this feeling of happiness."

I gawked at him, wondering how someone who had lost the will to fight or survive could bring happiness in someone else's life.

"Come home tonight, we will sort something out," I said walking out of the tunnel. He stood there smiling.

I had to grab his hand and drag him out. "We are just going to have a talk, Purab. Stop smiling." But he didn't.

He came home after 10:30pm, having told his mother that he was going to study with a friend.

KJ was certainly not happy seeing him, but Param let him inside the house.

It was I who did most of the talking while he beamed at me like I was his favourite porn star.

"So. You are fine with this?" I asked and he shook his head. "Purab?"

"Yeah," jumping up, he nodded. "Of course, I'm fine with this. No feelings, no attachment…"

"But that does not mean we can't we friends," I added and smiled. "I'm your friend and you are mine. You can tell me anything if you wish to."

"Of course," he nodded. "Same applies to you."

"Yes." I decided to lie down as my eyes were tired and close to shutting off.

His hand was almost inside my t-shirt when I said tiredly that I wanted to sleep. Without any protest, he understood and simply lay down next to me.

"You said that we can share, right?" he asked out of nowhere when my head was buried in the pillow.

Nodding with an effort, I looked at him, "You wanna talk to me?"

"No," he smiled removing his t-shirt which confused me. "I want you to talk to me. Who is that guy?" Throwing the t-shirt on the floor he stared into my eyes while mine turned moist. "The one who lives across from you? He is the same guy who broke your heart, right?"

I didn't answer for a while and he sensed my discomfort. "Only if you want to…"

"I want to know something before I answer your question," I said with a deadpan expression.

"What?" he asked in an amusing tone.

"About your father." Now his face turned pale just like mine had few seconds back and he refused to meet my eyes.

"What about him?" he asked stoically.

"Anything you would like to tell me about him." I said simply, checking his face for any sign of discomfort. "How do you remember him?"

"When he left my mother I was just 12. He didn't leave her because he was in love with someone else. He left her because he was never in love with her."

"It was a forced marriage?" I asked, wondering myself.

"Arranged marriage," he smiled despondently. "Quite close to forced marriage. Some couples do find love even in arranged marriages;

my mother said they never found their share of love. I'm not sure if they looked for it or not." He paused and continued, "Or never even tried to find it but they were never happy with each other and one day he just left."

"It must have been hard for you." I held his hand when I saw tears in his eyes.

"In the beginning," he nodded. "I only saw him as an absconding man and not as a father. But now," looking at me he shrugged, "I think I understand him. Why would a person want to continue a life which is making him miserable and wretched?"

I tried to picture Purab's dad. He had to be old, maybe an older version of Purab. But all I saw was Ahyan. Those words were applicable to Ahyan. Forced marriage. Arranged marriage. Miserable and wretched.

I could not hide the tears in my eyes after that. Purab thought his story had made me cry so he hugged me.

"I'm glad you don't see your dad as a villain," I smiled wiping my tears.

"Yeah, me too," he held my hand and kissed it gently. "So tell me your story…"

"What do you wanna know?" I asked firmly.

"Is it the same guy because of whom you are like this?" He asked and I did not understand what he actually meant. But I really didn't have the energy to ask.

"Yes, it is the same guy," I said staring at my nails. "He changed my life."

"It must be weird that he lives across from you." I choked a little at his words but didn't say anything. "But I barely ever see him come out of his flat."

"Yeah," I nodded. "He is not here for me. Only he knows why he is here."

"Do you love him?" he was staring deep into my eyes.

I looked up and stared into his beautiful eyes. "No. Neither of us loved each other ever and yet managed to damage each other's lives."

Chapter Seven

Next day when I returned from school I found Ahyan lying at our doorstep, tipsy. I politely asked him to move so I could get in but he wanted me to pick him up.

"What are you doing, Ahyan?" I roared and knew no one would hear me, not even him. "Why the fuck are you making things harder?"

He began laughing as if I had cracked a joke. I felt like kicking his balls but I waited patiently.

"I wanna talk to you," he said finally getting up clumsily holding on to the door. I could not believe my eyes; Ahyan so miserable that he needed something to support him to stand.

"What is it?" I asked once the door was unlocked. There was no way I could take him inside—KJ won't like it and Param would never enter the house if he found out he was here again.

"Can't I come inside?" he asked graciously which made me laugh but I merely shook my head.

"Please." Begging, he held my hand but I pushed it away. "Just for a few minutes. I need water."

"You stay here." I said opening the door. "And I will bring water for you."

"Where are your manners, Ria?" he mocked me. "You will offer me water at the door? What am I? A beggar?"

"Worse than that," I commented walking in and found him at my heels. Despite my protests, he got comfortable on the sofa.

I had to get him out before anyone walked in. Soon after offering him water I asked him what he wanted to talk to me about. He remained quiet, taking me in.

"If you have nothing to say, please get out," I finally said, keeping my rage barely in check.

"Where are your manners, Ria?" he asked again and I was so agitated that I wanted to break the glass on his head.

"My manners I shoved up your ass." I gritted my teeth while he kept gazing me. "Now, talk or get the fuck out of here."

"You seem to keep the little boy in your bed for so long," glaring me he got up, "but can't tolerate my sight for even a bit anymore, huh?"

"You son of a bitch." I shook my head. "This is not your business. I will keep whomever I want in my bed."

"Why?" he screamed loudly just like old Ahyan used to, making me jump. "Why? Why him!?"

"Then whom do you want me to fuck?" I asked laughing at him. "You?"

"Why not me?" he asked anger growing on his serene face. "Do you hate me so much?"

"Ahyan!" I cried, not able to control my tears. "You are married, Ahyan."

"Married," he gritted his teeth. "That fuck-all marriage my parents put me through…"

"It still does not change the fact that you are…"

"I know!" he screamed again, glaring at me. "I know I am married. But I still want you. I have always wanted you."

"What?" I whispered and sat down, not able to breathe.

"I don't know what I'm doing with my life." With those words he turned into a stone, analyzing his life. "I don't want this. I never wanted this in the first place."

"Then why did you agree to this marriage?" He was avoiding my eyes.

"I had to…"

"No, you didn't!" I said loudly and got his attention. "You could have spoken your mind. You could have said no, but you didn't have the fucking balls to deny anything to your family. You didn't have the fucking balls to tell me that you were already engaged when you were fucking me."

His face said everything he couldn't. It looked like someone had kicked his balls and simultaneously stabbed his heart repeatedly.

Ahyan could not move for a long time after that and looked pretty close to tears.

"You know…" he murmured in a heavy voice, "I'm sorry. I didn't know what…"

"You ruined my life," I said. "For your fun, you played with my emotions and my life."

"I was so confused," he put his fucked-up head in his palms and cried openly. "I could not understand what was the right thing to do."

"You knew what was right," I answered looking at him, his head still buried in his hands. "That is why you did not want to run away with me. That is why your father freaked out when my dad suggested we get married. You people knew all along."

"I swear, Ria," he got up and sat next to my feet. "I was so messed up in my head that I didn't know what I should have done. Please forgive me and come with me." He wrapped himself around my legs, tears streaking down his face. He looked so vulnerable, almost like a victim of some barbaric torture.

"No! Nothing matters now," I pushed him away from me. "Nothing can change now."

"What do you mean?"

"Please get out," I said politely, wiping my tears and walking silently to my room.

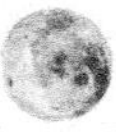

Purab wanted me to help him with his studies as his exam was nearing. I suggested he come to my place in the evening. KJ disliked the idea of me being Purab's *teacher* saying that he was just looking for ways to get in my pants. I smiled at him and said I didn't mind that either.

"Here," he passed me a giant book which I could barely hold. "Ask me the first question."

"Okay, um, tell me about globalization in detail," I read carefully and then looked at him.

He stared at me for full two minutes where I assumed he had forgotten the answer so I waited.

Finally, I cleared my throat, "Globalization is a process…"

"Shit!" he said banging his fist on the bed. "I knew this answer. It's just, I see you and forget everything."

"Then I will call Param to help you out," I suggested, closing the book with a loud thud.

"No, you stay here," he held on to my hand. "I will remember, just give me a minute."

I gave him more than a minute and he did know the answer very well.

While he studied, I got some food for us.

"What did you tell your mother?" I asked, placing the plate in front of him.

"Hmm," he looked at the items on the plate. *Puri* and *aloomatar* sabzi. His face lit up like a lantern. I frowned as I was used to eating them often, these being KJ's favorite.

"I said I'm staying at Amir's place, a friend of mine from college." He kept the book aside.

"Good," I said taking a small bite of the hot and delicious *puri*. "I hope your mother does not find out or…"

"Don't worry," he smiled earnestly, "she wouldn't. She is too happy that I'm going to college and studying again."

"Mother was saying that," he looked into my eyes timidly and then continued, "um, KJ's neighbour was wandering in our wing the other night. He looked heavily sloshed."

I stopped eating and shook my head slowly. "Did he get home safely?"

"Yeah," Purab nodded examining my face which I'm sure had worry written all over it. "Our neighbour helped him."

"Good," I barely whispered and started eating again.

"You sure you don't love him?" His interrogation never stopped. "You care for him so much."

"I don't love him and neither does he," I replied like a robot.

"How come love never came in between?" he threw another question at me and I know I should have been mad at him but I started wondering.

"Love was not meant for us." I stated staring at nothing as if in a trance.

"But you care for him so much and I'm sure even he does, deep down," Purab said.

I didn't answer but just raised my eyebrow and put a huge piece of *aloo* in my mouth.

"Do you feel like going back to him?" again Purab's eyes were scared to face me yet they had the courage to stare at me, expecting an answer.

How could I tell this 20-year-old boy that Ahyan was fucked-up in his marriage? Would he even understand any of this stuff? Would he ever understand Ahyan? But then I remembered how he supported his father that day.

"*Ya Amar,*" I spoke the words slowly and loudly playing with the *puri* in my hand and smiling at Purab.

"What does that mean?" asked the curious 20-year-old smiling at me.

I looked at his plate, he had already finished his dinner and I was still playing with my food.

"It's an Egyptian phrase and it means 'my moon'." I explained thinking about my moon. "Ahyan was always my moon and I was the wolf looking at him from a distance, craving for him and crying in silence. When I first saw him, I was bowled over and something told me I would never get him. That was the first time I realized that he was my moon. Even after having him I never had him completely; he was never mine, he was always someone else's."

"What about now?" he asked. "It does not look like he is happy with whoever he is. What if he asks you to be with him?"

"What rubbish!" I almost yelled, not wanting to hear the words Ahyan had uttered to me.

"What if god gives you a chance to be more than just a wolf?" His questions rained down on me. "Would you go with him if he asks you to?"

"Purab," I sighed, "that would be wrong. He is married."

He took my face in his hands and I stared at his cheerful face. "You are so great, I admire you."

"What?" I was baffled by his words which he didn't care to explain.

"Can I get more *puris*, please?" he asked smiling brightly. I shook my head reaching for his plate.

That day I got a surprise visit to my school from an awfully troubled Ahyan. He looked like ten men had beaten him close to death. I didn't know how I was supposed to react—scream at him, throw him out, and pretend I didn't know who that sad ass was?

I politely asked him to get the fuck out of my face and meet me later. But as usual, Ahyan didn't understand the words coming out of my mouth and waited for me outside the school till it was time for me to leave. He loitered all day like a street urchin and looking like one too.

I was so furious I yelled at him in front of everyone, hailed a cab and came home alone. He followed me in another cab, coming after me like a lost puppy.

"What do you want?" I spit the words out as we reached our floor. "Why the fuck can't you leave me alone?"

"I need to talk," he muttered removing the keys from his pocket to unlock the door.

Leaving the door open for me, he stepped inside. I stood there deciding what I was gonna do. Talk to him? Ignore him?

Before I could turn around and leave, not giving Ahyan a chance to present his side, he returned.

"Please." He offered his hand. My eyes fell on him and it seemed like nothing bad had ever happened. It felt like we were back in that storage room, fucking like bunnies.

I followed him inside quietly. I took the only vacant chair, others being occupied with clothes, papers, books.

Ahyan offered me water and I gulped it down as if it was neat vodka.

"So?" I said, prompting him.

"Did you think about what I had asked you the last time we were in the same room?"

"About what?" I asked a little confused.

He found it difficult to bring the words out and I understood what he was talking about. I wanted to torture him hence pretended to be clueless.

"You and I going away from here." He didn't look at me.

"You mean," I asked in mock confusion, "you and I running away from everyone?"

"Yes," he barely whispered.

"You, running away from your wife?" My temper was rising slowly which made him cringe. "That poor woman waiting for you somewhere. And I, running away from these nice people who saved my life?"

"I won't be running away, Ria," he finally looked at me with watery eyes. "We would be together. Don't you think that's important?"

"What is wrong with you, Ahyan?" I asked miserably. "When did you become *this* shameless and selfish? What has happened to you?"

"I don't know," he said shivering due to cold. "I just want to be somewhere where I can be sane, Ria. I can't take it anymore. This is killing me every day."

"What is?" I asked suddenly concerned as I had never seen him this disturbed before. "Ahyan?"

He got up from his seat and hugged me, his body shaking with his sobs as if someone had died. Well, something died. Our souls, our spirits, our willingness to be happy again.

"What is the matter, Ahyan?" I asked in a soothing tone. "You can tell me everything."

"I don't know, Ria," he said wiping his tears and sliding back to the floor. "It's like something is suffocating me, I feel like I'm drowning."

Those words brought tears to my eyes. That's how I felt when Ahyan got married.

"I just want to be happy; Ria.I cannot live in despair anymore. I have had enough being unhappy and making others unhappy too."

"I know what I go through every day." I sat down next to him. "I try to be happy but, in the end, all I'm left with is this hollow feeling deep inside me. Nothing gives me happiness. Nothing gives me hope. But I know if I will be with you, we will be together, we will figure something out. After all," he said looking into my glassy eyes, "no one understands me like you do."

"But Ahyan," I mumbled while he held my hand, "what about your wife?"

"I'm done making her unhappy." His words, said so seriously and so full of regret, it baffled me. "I could not keep her happy for a minute. I cannot continue doing that to her."

"And your job?" I asked wiping my tears.

"I don't have a job. They fired me because I was irresponsible."

"But you told KJ that your company shifted you here?" I asked and he shook his head.

"I lied," he answered, avoiding my gaze, "I lost my job long ago and decided to get away from my family. So I came here, I knew no one and no one knew me here..."

"But you found me," I murmured thinking how absurd it was. Destiny.

"And I'm so thankful," he whispered getting closer and holding my face in his large hands.

"You will come with me, Ria?" he whispered in my ear kissing the lobe slowly. I knew I was to push him away but I could not.

"I have to think about it, Ahyan," I whispered back and he kissed my cheek gently before moving to my lips. It was when his hands started moving all over, I pushed him away gently.

"Not now," I said. He looked heartbroken but agreed, smiling.

How could I ever escape Ahyan's questions, his inner darkness and his pleadings? My feelings for him had changed but I knew I could never leave him stranded as he did. Like me, I knew he was capable of doing something wretched to himself.

For days, I could not eat or sleep properly. Param noticed my mood swings, my discomfort, my sadness. I lied, saying it was that time of the month. But I knew I had to make a decision. What was I going to do? Enter into Ahyan's world as his mistress and abandon every shame? What about his wife? How could I ever erase her thought from my head?

On my way home few days later from school, I came across a *burqa* shop. I knew I should have gone home early as it was going to snow. But I entered the shop shivering with cold and trepidation.

Everything inside the shop was so unfamiliar to me, yet I felt I belonged there. There were many ladies shopping along with their husbands or children. An old man with an orange beard asked me kindly what I wanted.

I looked at him, his eyes were different, and he had kindness filled in them. Shaking my head, I just went around looking at the *burqas* kept on different racks. One of the *burqas* caught my eye; it was simple, just like the one Ahyan had borrowed from his uncle for me. I asked a young boy to show me the piece.

He brought it down and started talking about its material and what not. I hardly paid attention to his words and went to the changing room.

Five minutes later, I was sobbing with the *burqa* still in my hands. I was clutching it like it was a precious stone for me. I was reminded of the past, every single detail. How the hell was I to make a decision with this mind?

I wanted to talk to someone, someone who could understand me. Purab had his exams and I did not want to disturb him.

Param came to my rescue. I hadn't left the trial room, clutching the *burqa* and crying. Not knowing what else to do, I called him. He got me out and apologized to the old man with the orange beard who had a concerned look on his face.

"Are you okay?" Param asked. We were seated on the stairs of a small church which was shut for the day.

"Yes," I whispered, hiccupping. He hugged me as it slowly started snowing.

"This is because of him, right?" His voice was stern. "What did he do now?"

"He wants me to go away with him," I answered wiping my tears which weren't stopping.

"And?" Param looked at me with a concerned look. "You want to go with him?"

"I don't know," I replied. "I don't know anything, Param."

"What do you want?" he asked not looking at me but at the ground where snowflakes were falling slowly. "If he is what you want then you must go, Ria."

"What?" I was shocked because I knew how much Param hated Ahyan.

"Your happiness is what matters the most," he said smiling lightly, knowing he had surprised me. "You have been unhappy for so long. It is time you leave it behind."

"And his wife?" I immediately asked with a lump in my throat. "What about her happiness?"

"I don't think she is in anyway happy with that man." He said not knowing how true it was.

"But Param," I looked around us, at the trees which were turning white, "is it ethical to steal another woman's husband?"

"No," he looked into my eyes. "Never. But I don't think Ahyan is anyone's to steal."

"Well, still, it doesn't matter," I said my eyes getting moist again. We were shivering now. "If it is unethical, it is unethical. Ahyan's mental state does not make any difference."

"The decision is yours, Ria." He held my hand and it comforted me. "Don't worry about KJ. I will make him understand."

"Thanks." I hugged him smiling, despite my tears.

Chapter Eight

I could not escape my thoughts which were giving me sleepless nights. Param promised to keep our meeting a secret until I was ready to make a decision. I was looking out of the window at the deserted street. Again, I had the same vision I once had on a drunken night, many days ago.

I saw us, Ahyan and I, standing near a mosque laughing happily, holding hands. Could this be our future? Can we ever be that happy after all the pain?

I was so deep in my thoughts that I didn't notice my phone was ringing. It was Purab, crying on the other side. He sounded like a baby who was bruised.

"What happened, Purab?" I asked in my motherly voice

"I had a fight with mom again." he sulked. "Can I come to you now?"

"Yes, of course," I got up from the chair. "Where are you?"

"Outside your door," I heard him say and I ran for the door. Both KJ and Param were fast asleep in their rooms.

As soon as I opened the door he jumped on me and hugged me tightly. I took him to my room where he continued crying like a baby.

"What happened?" I asked again bringing him some water and tissues. "Tell me everything."

"It was my last day of exams so I came home late." Purab started his tale as the dogs outside began howling. "When I reached home I saw my mother had found some of my old stash."

"What was that old stash still doing in your house?" I tried not to yell but could not help it. "You told me you were clean."

"Yes, but I didn't exactly stop selling them," he added regretfully as I shook my head in dismay.

"Why?" I said a little angrily which resulted in more tears. "Um, sorry," I held his hand and spoke in a soothing tone. "What happened next?"

"I know it is wrong and I'm not supposed to do it but I just needed little cash so I thought..." he broke down and I held him. He hugged me tight and started howling like the dogs outside.

"I won't ever do it, I told her, I promised her but she does not believe me. She kicked me out again." I caressed his hair slowly as his tears fell on my bare shoulders. He spoke, breathing with difficulty, "I really don't know what I was supposed to do. I disappointed her again."

"It's okay," I replied after sometime. "She will forget everything. She is mad at you now. Tomorrow will be better, I promise."

"She said I'm stupid and that I have made her life hell just like my father did." I busied myself wiping his tears. "She does not need me, so I yelled at her that I too didn't need her."

"But that's not true, you both need each other."

"How could she do this to me on my birthday?" he said rubbing his eyes. "I'm sorry. I was going to call you after my exam. My initial plan was to spend my birthday with you but my friends took me out."

"That's okay," I smiled, kissing his cheek. "Happy Birthday."

"Thank you," he replied smiling slightly. "Ria?"

"Hmm?"

"Do you think I'm stupid?" he asked suddenly. "Do you think I have ruined my life and causing my mom trouble?"

"No," I shook my head. "You are not stupid and you aren't causing any trouble, to anyone. You are the sweetest boy ever."

"Thank you," he grinned and kissed my lips. "I don't know what I would do without you."

"Me too," I replied without thinking as he held my hand.

"Promise me you will never leave me." I didn't even get a chance to answer as he again hugged me. "I would die if you ever left me."

What? Why did two men who were not in love with me want me in their lives? What was I supposed to do? Choose Ahyan or Purab? Choose the grown up with the mind of a little boy or the little boy himself?

Purab slept with me that night as he had nowhere to go. I too found some company and respite in his embrace. He slept like a little boy clutching his toy—me.

Was I really a toy? Did these men ever think what I wanted? Did they ever ask me what would bring *me* happiness? What if I did not want either of them? What if I did not want anyone at all?

In the morning, KJ opened the door to find me and Purab sleeping in a tight embrace. I got up because of his loud prayers.

"When did he get here?" KJ asked just as Param got out of his room yawning.

"Last night," I yawned too. "Was really messed up. His mom kicked him out so please don't be hard on him."

"Whose mom kicked whom out?" Param asked me sitting on the couch looking for the TV remote.

"Purab's," I murmured and vanished inside the washroom.

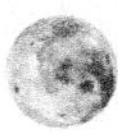

Few days passed and Ahyan started getting restless; he wanted me to make a quick decision. I was not even thinking about it anymore as the very thought of me and Ahyan turned my guts in a knot. But I had to tell him something. I would be lying if I said there weren't days when I believed that we might find some happiness after all. But on most days my mind kept screaming only one word: *Wrong*.

It kept yelling the word over and over again until I knew we could never be together. Some say that in great stories a mistress is always remembered and not the wife. But what's the point of even remembering a mistress as she will always be remembered as a mistress and not as the wife?

Purab went back to his mother's place as he promised her he would never even talk about drugs. He was going for interviews and seriously looking for a job.

Dressed in a white crisp shirt and black pants, he met me that day as I was already late for school.

"Wow," I laughed looking at him, "You look decent. Very smart and handsome too."

"Thank you," he blushed. "By the way, Param told me about that guy," he said awkwardly, "about how you might go back to him."

"Oh!" I murmured.

"You will go back to him? Which means you are leaving?" He sounded mournful.

"I don't know, Purab," I replied miserably. "I have not a decision yet."

"Before you make any decision I just wanted to say that I…"

"What?" I asked when he didn't finish his sentence.

"Nothing. First, you make a decision then I will let you know, and remember," he said looking into my eyes adoringly, something Ahyan had never done, "I only want your happiness."

"And I only want your happiness and for you to succeed, Purab," I smiled and wished him luck for his interview.

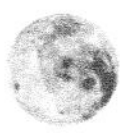

It was the last day of school and everyone was in a festive mood. I felt suffocated amongst the laughter and the cheerful people so I made an excuse and left early.

Param was craving for donuts since past few days so I decided to stop by a café and buy him some. I came across a one called Euphoria which I had never visited before and thought of exploring the place.

It had been snowing for the past few days and the temperature was dropping. I bought myself some coffee and sat on a stool near the window. Euphoria was a typical café which attracted a lot of young people. There were windows everywhere which were shut due to the cold. The place was dimly lit giving it a gloomy look.

I looked at the couch which was placed at the far end of the café. Two girls and a few boys were sitting close to each other and laughing. Suddenly, one of the boys looked at me and smiled. He looked so much like Purab. I diverted my eyes towards the window and focused on the snowfall.

I felt someone touch my leg, more like shaking it. A toddler dressed in white clothes had found his way to me while his mother sat on the table nearby. I picked him up and looked at his kohl-eyes. My eyes filled with tears as he looked just like little Ahyan. I had seen his childhood pictures and he had the same innocent face, big kohl-rimmed eyes.

"Saqib?" I heard a woman's voice who was dressed in a black *burqa*.

She tried to take the child from me but he was not ready to let go. He clutched my scarf tightly in his tiny fists.

"I'm so sorry," she said keeping her large bag near the window and grabbing her son from me.

"That's okay," I smiled as the boy started throwing a tantrum. She looked like she had been crying a lot.

"Saqib *jaan*," she comforted the child but he started crying. Finally, she gave him a toy from her bag, successfully diverting his attention with the tiny doll.

She kept juggling with her bag while I sipped coffee staring at the little kid who had forgotten about me. Her purse fell and I saw Ahyan's picture in it. My heart stopped beating right there. I looked at her, the kid and the picture. She grabbed her purse and shoved it inside the bag.

She pulled out a box of cookies and fed her son. I struggled with the toughest decision: to talk to her or not. Even if I spoke to her, what would I tell her?

She already looked so miserable. She looked more sorrowful than me. This is what Ahyan does to people around him, I thought as I finished my coffee. She was pretty, fair, blue-eyed beauty some might call. And without those sad eyes and dark circles, I assumed she might look even more beautiful. But there was one thing I could not help but notice. She was no match for Ahyan. The way I always felt that I was no match for Ahyan since he was so beautiful and handsome at the same time. His wife too was ordinary in front of him. I always thought his parents might find a girl who was much better looking than their son. But maybe no one was better looking than Ahyan. And more fucked-up either.

I decided I had no balls to face her, and the kid's face was haunting me. I thought the best thing would be to just leave.

But her phone rang and she picked it up with shivering hands. She hardly spoke a word, mutely listening to whoever was speaking. Ahyan's son was now looking out of the window, mesmerized.

"I know I made a mistake by coming here alone but I know I will find him." She sounded quite close to tears. "Yes. I asked someone if Ahyan lives here. They said he does but he is not home."

Wow, so Ahyan chickened out or did he not open the door?

"How can I come back without him?" Now she was crying and the boy looked at his mother with a concern only young ones can display. "I'm sorry, *bhaijaan*, but I will bring him with me. Hello…hello?"

She threw the phone inside the bag.

"Are you looking for Ahyan?" I asked without thinking. I could not bear to see her crying miserably like that. I had to do something.

"Do you know him?" she asked wiping the tears as the kid smiled at me.

Every second spent with him flashed in front of my eyes in that instant. I had to hide every emotion and answer her.

"I'm his neighbour." I looked into my white cup as I said that white lie.

"Do you know where he is?" she asked again, sounding a little hopeful.

"Um, no," I shook my head. "We hardly see him come out of the house or go anywhere."

"Oh." Her eyes filled with tears. I suddenly realized it was Beth Hart's 'Caught Out In Rain' playing in the background.

"Don't cry," I muttered wanting to cry with her.

"What else should I do?" she asked me as if I had answers. "I waited outside the house for hours. Nobody opened the door; no one knows where he is. Where should I look for him?"

"Look, erm," I stammered as I didn't know her name and had no idea what was I supposed to call her.

"Oh, I'm Fareeda," she said wiping her nose with a tissue, "and this is Saqib."

"Um, Fareeda, did you try calling him?" I saw a tinge of anger on her face.

"He has not been using that number since he left and I don't know his other number or should I say *numbers*," she snorted in anger as I looked down in shame. I knew Ahyan's other numbers; he used to message me from them sometimes.

"But what exactly happened, Fareeda?" I asked as if I knew her more than Ahyan.

"He got away from me," she said with a deadpan expression while her son smiled at something outside. "Marriage was strangling him."

"I'm sorry," I could not meet her sorrowful eyes.

"Oh, no," she laughed sadly. "It's okay. He has done worse things to me than just leave without notice."

"What do you mean?" I asked firmly, not able to handle my shock and rage. "Did he hit you?"

Hearing that she quickly looked at her *burqa* as if checking for any scars which might be visible.

"He would sleep with other women, then come home and beat me."

"What?" I barely whispered and willed the tears to stop.

"Did you ever see any women go to his room?" she asked curiously. "You live next to him, no?"

"Um," I felt like I was getting strangled by her questions. "No. We hardly ever see him."

Fareeda stayed quiet for a while, running her hands through her kid's hair and crying silently.

"It's all my fault," she said in a choked voice. "I never gave him any happiness. Whatever I did, whatever I said, nothing ever brought any happiness on his face. He was always," she stopped, trying to think of a word, "empty. He was always trapped in something; he needed to be rescued, but I could not rescue him."

"Sometimes I heard him crying alone at night in the washroom or in the balcony." I closed my eyes to stop the tears. "He never told me what was happening inside his head. Whenever I asked the reason for his erratic moods, he would beat me up. Once he pushed me when I was 8months pregnant and you know what's the worst thing? He wasn't sorry. He simply stared at me as if he was high on drugs..." She gasped softly. "His father slapped him so hard. It drove Ahyan mad."

"That day made me realize I didn't know who the actual victim was," she said as I wiped the tears from my shocked face, "I or my husband? I didn't know my husband at all even after so many months. I have no idea who that man is. I don't know where he is. I came here all alone without telling anyone. Everyone is so mad at me. My parents, his parents. My brothers are coming to take me home. But you tell me," she asked again, sobbing, as Saqib looked worriedly at his mother, "how can I go without him? My little boy has no idea where his father is."

"I think you should go back," I said after a lot of thinking. "When I see Ahyan, I will tell him to go back to you."

"Really?" her hopeful eyes spoke more to me than those words.

"Yes," I was going to live up to my words. "I promise. You should leave with your brothers."

"But do you think he will listen to you?" she asked staring at me like I was a stranger. Which I was but only to her. "He never listened to his own people…"

"Don't worry," I assured her. "He will have to listen to us. My friend is his landlord. Once he kicks him out he will have to come back to you."

She held my hand and thanked me as Saqib smiled innocently at his toy.

<h1 style="text-align:center">Chapter Nine</h1>

As soon as I reached home both KJ and Param knew something was wrong. I tossed the donuts at Param and told KJ to kick Ahyan out. It brought a smile on Param's face; he knew I had made my decision.

"What happened, Ria?" worriedly KJ looked at me, at Param and then back at me.

"Will tell you later," I said and marched to Ahyan's house.

Knocking on the door for the second time, I stood outside as KJ and Param stared at me from our house.

"Ahyan," I screamed angrily, "Open up. It's me, Ria."

Ahyan appeared at the door after sometime, looking even more miserable. He was stinking of liquor.

I closed the door shut and stood in that messy apartment facing the pathetic man for whom I had destroyed my life.

"I met Fareeda today," I said gritting my teeth.

He looked vacantly at me as if he was high on something. Fareeda was right.

"Fareeda, your wife," I yelled and he looked away, in shame or anger I could not tell.

"You were home when she was knocking on the door, weren't you?" I questioned and he sat down quietly on the chair, scratching his head. "Why didn't you open the door, Ahyan?"

He didn't say anything and pretended as if he had gone deaf. I wondered how a person could be so heartless that he would drive away his wife and infant son.

"Do you even love that kid?" I asked and Ahyan looked at me furiously.

"Of course, I love him!" he barked at me. "He is my son."

"Then why didn't you open the door?" I yelled louder than him as I pictured Fareeda standing outside with Saqib and knocking helplessly.

"Because I did not want to see her," he screamed back at me clutching his head and slipping to the cold floor.

"Why, Ahyan?" I sat down too and pulled his arm away from his face so he could see me, face me and look me in the eye. "What has she done to you?"

He looked at me blankly.

"You are the one who ruined her life. You." I said instead, crying for Fareeda. "You are the one who has given her scars which she is going to carry till her death. This is what you do, Ahyan." His eyes were swimming in unshed tears. "You ruin people's life. First, you ruined my life and now you ruined Fareeda's. This is what you are good at, aren't you?"

"Yes," he bellowed. "This is what I do. I ruin people's life. I mar their happiness and sanity. But who asked you to be a part of my life? I didn't tell you to run away; neither did I force Fareeda to marry me!"

I could not stop looking at him in astonishment. How could he say something like that? He still didn't think it was his fault the chaos was in our lives. Was he so bewildered to see the reality? Or he was still thinking about himself? I don't think I could call Ahyan heartless anymore. He had reached a different level of insanity.

"What have you become, Ahyan?" I cried not believing a man could change so much, that life could fuck someone to that extent.

"You know what I have become," he answered plainly wiping the tears off his face. "Where is she?"

"I told her to leave," I replied stoically. "Her brothers came to pick her up."

"How did she find out I was here?"Ahyan asked me but I decided not to tell him the pain Fareeda went through to get to him. How she called each and every friend of his.

"Why don't you go and ask her?" I said coldly staring deep into his dead eyes.

"You know I won't do that," he muttered angrily thinking he could scare me.

"She told me everything, Ahyan," I said even more angrily. "How you hit her, how you tortured her, how you slept with other women."

He could not look at me for a while after that so I asked him to look at me, face me.

"You thought I was going to be monogamous after marriage?" he laughed at my face when he should have felt guilty. "She never made me happy."

"*Shut up!*" I shouted slapping him hard. "Shut the fuck up. Shut up. Shut up. Shut up, Ahyan!"

Never in my life had I imagined that I could scare Ahyan but he looked terrified of me.

"What happiness did you give her, you asshole?" I asked pulling against his collar as he stared at me. "You are such a disgrace. Allah is watching everything, remember that," I finally left his collar as he sat there mutely, going back into a trance.

"Get out of my life and this house right now!" I stood up slowly as his eyes followed me. "And if you are still a man and got balls, divorce her. Leave her, let her live in peace, and then you can go fuck other women as well as your disgraceful life."

"Ria," he murmured getting up. "Don't ask me to leave, please…"

"You have one hour to get the fuck out of here," I ordered as he held my arms. But I was strong enough to push him back. That was it; that was the last time we touched each other.

"Goodbye, Ahyan," I said, my heart heavy and finally ending that chapter forever.

"Ria," he moaned, eyes filling with tears but I felt nothing for him. I left him alone to cry and deal with his life.

That was the last time I ever saw Ahyan.

I was done with him once and for all; I decided I had to live for myself now. He had done enough damage to himself, me and Fareeda. It's not like I didn't care about him. Much had changed since I first saw him standing outside that door. That was the time when I only wanted to hurt him, maim him. But I realized he was already broken, so how the fuck do you break something which is already broken? I was done being unhappy. I decided, like Fareeda, I too had to start my life anew. Unfortunately, Ahyan was not going to be a part of it anymore.

I knew I was not going to regret the decision. I was doing something good. I was thinking about bettering my life. I was thinking about me, I was thinking about Fareeda. Ahyan's only mistake was that he was no longer in my thoughts.

I still wished in some other time, some other life, we could still be together. We deserved to be together at least once. Because we were so eccentric together than even the universe would have no frigging balls to handle us.

A week after Ahyan left, Purab confessed his love for me. At first, I thought it was a joke but then he told me he was madly in love with me. I explained to him that we could never be together due to innumerable reasons which were hard to explain. But the boy was so adamant.

After a few months, even KJ accepted him which made things worse for me. He chased me, stalked me everywhere I went. Even after getting a good job, he found time to drop at our place unannounced just to see me.

I decided to I needed to move and I applied everywhere for a job. For five years, I worked in Darjeeling, Calcutta, and Bangalore and then came back to Shimla. He chased me everywhere I went, changing his job and life.

Eventually, I gave in telling him that he won and I could not ignore him anymore. I remember that day very well. We were standing right in front of that church where I had sat crying with Param, many lifetimes ago. Purab grabbed me and kissed me in front of everyone. It was awful because people were not used to it.

His mother abandoned him, knowing he was involved with me. This time Purab didn't cry or wail, he was a grown man now, but I felt bad. After we got together, his father called him to Canada to help him with the business.

A few months later, we moved to Canada and started living-in together. Purab's father accepted me happily which made him even happier. Param too shifted to Canada after he got engaged to his boyfriend, John, who was a Canadian.

It was during Param's engagement that I found out I was pregnant. We flew KJ out to share the happy news and to also look after me. He found a job at an Indian store helping some Singh family look after their business when he was not babysitting me.

My father promised me that he would visit me once the baby came. My mother was still furious with me and when she learned I was knocked up before marriage, that too by a younger guy, she swore to never see me. Aditya left Bhumi and ran away with his ex-girlfriend from college. That said a lot about my brother. He was nothing but a deceiver. The picture he showed the real world about himself was a deception. But ultimately, his actions brought out the truth.

Epilogue

It was a lovely evening. Purab and Param were talking to someone about the final wedding arrangements as I decided to take a walk in the park close to the wedding hall. Param was getting married in 24 hours and was nervous as hell.

I saw a boy running out of the park as his mother came shouting behind him. "Saqib!"

Saqib looked to be 6-7 years old, I guessed. He still looked so much like Ahyan.

Handsome face, playful eyes and tall just like his father. Fareeda looked much younger than the last time I saw her. She immediately recognized me and walked towards me with an open smile.

"How are you?" she asked, first looking at me and then my big belly.

"I'm good. How are you and Saqib?" I asked returning her smile.

"Happy," she replied looking at her son talk to some white guy. "Finally, happy."

"So, you moved here?" I asked curiously and she shook her head.

"No. I live in California with my aunt," she informed and I was thrilled that she got away from everyone. "I'm here to meet my aunt's friends. After Ahyan divorced me, almost everyone abandoned me. My maternal aunt never had kids of her own and she always treated me like her daughter. She called me here." While she continued, I was glad that Ahyan had listened to me.

"…I work here with an Indian hairstylist. Whenever you come to California," she removed a card from her purse, "do visit our salon."

"Yeah, sure," I accepted her card. "So, where is Ahyan?"

"I don't know," she replied casually and I could not hide the disappointment on my face. "Haven't spoken to him in four years. Someone told me he was in Hyderabad last year. Allah knows." She shrugged.

"Okay," I tried to smile as Saqib came running to his mother.

Fareeda asked if he remembered me which was quite stupid since he was a baby then.

"No," Saqib replied smiling politely at me. That smile which reminded me so much of Ahyan, the way he would smile when he found something amusing. I couldn't erase him from my eyes.

"Say thank you to aunty, she helped us a lot," Fareeda told her little boy who reached my shoulders.

"Thanks a lot, aunty," he said kissing my cheek.

I was taken aback and Fareeda scolded him for his bad manners.

Shaking her head she laughed. "You know today's kids."

"Yeah," I nodded. And he was Ahyan's son so I shouldn't be surprised, I thought.

"Is that your husband?" she asked looking over my shoulders at the hall where Purab was standing and looking at me.

"Um, he is my boyfriend," I replied and waved at him. Param emerged from the hall talking loudly on phone in Hindi which meant it was KJ on the other end.

"Good," she smiled. "That's good too. All the best to you and your partner. I wish you become great parents."

"Yeah, thanks," I accepted her wishes as Purab and I needed it. We weren't showing each other but were very nervous about parenting. KJ assured he would be with us but still it gave us sleepless nights.

We bid goodbyes and I stood there looking at her and Saqib walk away from me.

"Hey," Param touched my arm. "Who was that?"

"Ahyan's ex-wife," I replied walking with him.

"Wow, she left him?" he asked, thrilled. "Oh, by the way, KJ is really fussing over these rituals. Please help me! I have asked Purab to talk to him."

I looked at Purab who was on phone with KJ, explaining something to him. He had changed so much over the years. From that boy who cried on my shoulders, he was going to become the father of my child.

And Ahyan, only god knew where he was. But I prayed wherever he was, he was happy. He too deserved it.

Param sprinted towards Purab and they both were now talking loudly with KJ on the phone. I looked up at the sky; the moon was slowly appearing. But what about my moon?

I could never see Ahyan and deep down I did not even want to see him. I was very happy with Purab. But Ahyan was my moon. I could only look at him from a distance but never touch him. He was my moon and I was his wolf; I could cry for him but would never make him mine. He wasn't even Fareeda's. He was no one's. Perhaps he was better this way.

Looking at the moon in the sky I remembered my moon for the last time. *"Ya Amar!"*

Made in the USA
Monee, IL
07 July 2026